Martin —
Thought ; got a kick out of this ...
Kevin

The McGill Way

By R.K. McGuire

For Laura, my best friend.

In memory of my cousin, Pat McGill

Part I

Southfork

Horse and rider moved steadily along the road towards the distant town. The late spring morning sun was rising and warming behind them. It was an altogether pleasant moment and the rider smiled as he whistled bits of an old Irish ditty he'd learned from his mother. It was a sad ancient song but the melody was pretty and put him in mind of happy memories.

It had been a long, lonely winter in the line shack up north in the hills. His task had been to keep the cows from wandering too far north and keep an eye out for the

predators hunting too far south. There had been

considerable rifle work in those snowbound months,

encouraging him to figure that he could easily put a notch

in a squirrel's ear from three hundred yards. He was still

a little surprised at how tasty the black bear had been.

The spring roundup was over and it had seemed

like a good time to move on. The cowboy was tired of the

outfit and the nasty old jasper that ran it so he collected

his pay and set off down the road in pursuit of another

future. Ambling along the trail on this beautiful morning

he knew that it was not the best time to think ahead in a

serious fashion. First he would need a barber and a bath,

followed by drink and food and maybe some female

companionship. He mused that he might well wake up in

a week with empty pockets and a headache. At that point

he would need a job. The cowboy shook his head as these

honest thoughts born out of experience were threatening his buoyant mood.

"Jack," he said aloud, "you haven't got to the party yet and already it's a headache and a bad memory!" Instead, Jack corralled his thoughts to the town ahead and the pretty girl that might be waiting there. He thought about the girl last summer over in Black Rock and shuddered with a mighty stirring. Then he laughed fit to spook the horse as he thought that his awakening might not be described as mighty by anyone but that girl or one engaged in like enterprise.

She'd gotten prettier and more buxom as the romance progressed and kept his glass full as she hung on his every word. She'd listened to his chatter for three days and took care of all his other needs as well. He walked away with some loose change and a sack of sandwiches she'd made or fetched. He'd felt more dead than alive, wrung out like an ole dishrag. He also felt sort of peaceful like and calm and the whole event had been a gosh darn good memory to go over now and again during those lonely months up in the hills.

The town was upon him now and the horse had slowed as if to take in a long drink of the sights of a dusty little frontier town. Jack considered the day and night ahead and urged his mount towards the hitch rail in front of the livery barn.

As he sat there watching the main street in the mid morning moment he heard three gunshots closely spaced. Shortly Jack saw two masked men carrying pistols and saddlebags running out the front door of the bank. Everyone else on the street was frozen in place as the robbers moved towards their horses. Jack was thinking as he watched the gunman in action that they might have had a couple of stiff drinks for breakfast.

There was a sudden yell as a stout old fella with a star carrying a double barreled shotgun lurched out of the jailhouse doorway and headed up the boardwalk and closer to the bank that was on the other side of the road from the jail. The lawman was yelling to get the attention of the robbers. They reacted by moving apart and raising their pistols. They did not seem very intimidated as the old man thumbed the hammers back. He fired one load a little high and between them, which cleaned all the glass out of the front door of the bank.

Jack was surprised at the sheriff's choice as he was left with one barrel and two targets with pistols at the ready. The robbers hesitated only a second before exchanging a look and then a laugh as they triggered the pistols. The sheriff appeared to be hit at least five times before he went backwards through the window of the hardware store. The discharge from the second barrel of the shotgun blew a large hole in the store's awning over the boardwalk.

Jack sat on his horse watching the melee and sorting out his loyalties. The robbers were laughing and looking everywhere for hostile reactions as they got mounted with the saddlebags and pointed their horses in the direction of open country and Jack.

He was thinking of high mountain meadows and trout streams and summer romances. He was also thinking that life was short and that all this was none of his affair. Still and all, he felt like killing these two characters just because they needed killing. It didn't appear like anyone else was going to step up here. Jack flipped a coin in his mind and watched it land on its edge. He smiled and pulled his rifle as he dismounted, throwing the reins around the hitchrail.

Jack stepped forward and went down on one knee as he laid the rifle across the rail. He levered a round into the firing chamber and sighted down the barrel and along the street. The lead rider took notice of the cowboy's actions and snapped off a shot which smashed into the wall of the livery barn as Jack squeezed off a careful round that hit the outlaw in the middle of his chest and drove him right off the charging horse.

The falling rider shied the second horse and the remaining outlaw fought for control with one hand as he tried to draw a bead on Jack. The cowboy was ready but took the time to see the perfect heart shot before he pulled the trigger. The dead man seemed to lift from the horse before he fell to roll in the dust of the road.

Jack rose and grabbed his reins as he rounded the hitchrail. He held the rifle out in front and trailed his horse as he walked into the path of the onrushing horses.

He waved the rifle, pushing the two horses back towards the livery barn. They slowed and stopped by the rail. Jack stowed the rifle and collected the reins of the outlaws' horses to loop them around his saddle horn for the time being. He pushed back between the horses to have a look at the saddlebags he'd seen carried from the bank. The gold coins and paper money he saw in those bags almost took his breath away.

It was enough to turn a fella's head. Jack's imagination soared into full flight with visions of women and clothes, cigars and horses and hotels and on and on. He glanced towards the bank and realized that he could live a whole different life with that kind of money. The temptation was nagging at him that he could take the horses and money and ride like hell and, likely, get clean away. So, he mused, it was a choice. Even though today he would choose to return the money to the bank he would remember this distracting moment. It was something to think long and hard about another day as he checked the reins on his saddle horn and picked up his own reins to head up the street to the bank. For now, he suspected that he would be the hero of the day in this little town.

A lot of memories came back as he moved slowly up the street. He had been working with cattle for one outfit or another since he was fifteen. It was really all that he had ever known, at least since he had left the family farm in Missouri and headed west after the war. Cattle ranches and cattle drives filled the entire space of all those years and now he was almost twenty-five years old. In these few moments he realized that he was might be done with all that. Maybe it was time to try something else.

He reckoned that he could always go back to the cowboy's life. He could do that in his sleep. Maybe there were some other things to try his hand at, perhaps like shooting bad guys. It would appear that he had some talent for that right from the get-go. Course it was also true that it might have gone the other way and it might be him stretched out on the street, all twisted and bloody and dead.

He had never killed a man before and was curious about his attitude about that killing. It had happened very fast and he had been very deliberate about it, like shooting deer or other in the forest. He had seen the dead, especially in Missouri during the war and after and in cow town gunfights and ranch and trail accidents. And now here he had visited that final event on these two fellas and their lives were over because of him. One might say that the old fat sheriff had been swiftly avenged but also no doubt that he was still quite dead.

Walking towards the bank he could see a couple of fellas looking in the window of the hardware store at the remains of the lawman. Jack noticed out of the corners of his eyes that people were coming out of doors up and down the street. He could feel himself getting a good deal of attention as he walked slowly towards the front of the bank.

No one was coming out of that door so he stopped 20 feet from what was left of the door and yelled, "Hello, anyone in the bank?"

A tall, slender and bookish looking fella stepped into the doorway. He carried a rifle at port arms but he said nothing. He stood there and stared at Jack and didn't seem all that friendly.

Jack felt a bit confused by the lack of welcome but pressed on, "Howdy, partner. My name is Jack McGill and I believe that I have recovered some money that belongs to you."

The banker was looking Jack up and down and said, "It's been a bad day and I don't know you, mister. I saw you at the livery with a rifle and thought that you might be one of them that robbed us. That was quite a shock when you killed them and then headed back this way…"

Jack interrupted, "What the hell's matter with you, mister. I just rode into town and shot the bad guys and rescued your money and brought it right here to your door. And your thanks is to start to wave that damned rifle in my face. That's a hell of a way to show your gratitude."

The banker pointed the rifle at the floor and stepped forward. "Don't judge me too harshly, mister, as I am really fit to be tied. The bank's been robbed, the town doctor's down on the floor in there bleeding his life away, the sheriff is shot to pieces and surely dead and it gets worse. The dead thief in the rain slicker is, or was, the son and only offspring of a cattleman by the name of Hank Wilson who is the richest and most powerful rancher in this part of the country.

"Among other things, Wilson is the biggest customer of my bank. I can't imagine what he is going to do when he finds out that his only son has been killed here today." His voice dropped a little here. "I mean, the son, Harold, Jr., was a real waste of his ma's bearing time, just the worst excuse for a man. But his old lady is dead and this is the only son. He shot the town doctor during the robbery when ole Doc recognized him even with the mask and called him out. So, no offense to you, mister, and my heartfelt thanks. You can believe absolutely that we are as grateful as we can be for what you done. I hope you can see better now why I was so at a loss or words a minute ago. Our little world has just been turned upside down by that young jackass and now rescued by your timely actions."

Jack was able to grin finally and approached the hitch rail to wind the rein around it. He turned to push through the trailing horses and retrieve the saddlebags. He then walked over with his right mitt out to greet the tall banker.

"My name is Tolliver, Jim Tolliver, and I am glad to make your acquaintance, McGill," he said as he shook Jack's hand. Jack noticed the softer and ink stained hand of the banker though in truth he had already decided that this Tolliver seemed like a pretty good sort of a fella. He was just a guy between an angry bull and the side of a red barn, but then he did have all that money back. Jack couldn't help but think that his recent decision to ride back into town instead of heading for the hills with the money was a decision that he might have reason to revisit. But what was done was done so he handed the two saddlebags to Tolliver and followed him into the bank.

An older man lay in a pool of blood in front of the teller's counter. He was breathing with great difficulty as his head was cradled in the blood-soaked lap of a frantically sobbing young woman. Jack stopped in his tracks as the old man gave a great shudder and died. The girl let out a loud cry and sobbed helplessly. Jack was sure that even at that terrible moment he had never seen or imagined another woman that could hold a candle to this girl's beauty. It was a long moment that would be seared into Jack's memory forever.

Then the moment was over and a young man in business clothes was trying to console the beautiful girl with Tolliver leaning forward in support but the girl seemed to be oblivious to them, capable only cradling her father's head in her lap and weeping. It appeared that she might be falling into complete shock.

Others people were now pushing into the bank behind Jack. The demeanor of the newcomers turned solemn very quickly as they took in the damage, particularly the dead man. One man turned on his heel back through the broken door to yell, apparently at some woman to hurry up and get into the bank. The sight of that young woman crying was enough to scare the heck out of almost any man. No one moved or said much but more people, including a couple of handsome older women, pushed through the bottleneck at the door and fanned out into the bank. The two women made a beeline for the young woman who disappeared from view as someone threw a coat over the dead man. Volunteers stepped up to give the dead man a ride to the mortician's place.

One big, roughly dressed guy turned to Jack, " That was quite a piece of shooting there, young fellow. Cool as a cucumber you were with those two guys riding down on you like that and spraying lead all over the place. Are you some kind of peace officer?"

Jack shook the hand he was offered while he shook his head. "No, I'm just a cow puncher on the move. I rode in minding my own business looking for a cold beer and a new job when I noticed the ruckus and decided to lend a hand."

"Well, we sure are obliged to you, mister, since most of us have money in this here bank. However, there is at least one devilish detail here and that is the fact that the first fella you shot and killed is the only son of the most powerful rancher in this part of the territory. Old man Wilson is also probably the hardest man hereabouts and no matter the whys and wherefores, what happened here is going to make him plumb crazy."

Jack realized that everyone in the place was looking at him now except for the three women who were going out the door. No one butted in to contradict that last thought.

Tolliver was still standing right handy by with the bags of money and he nodded in assent. "Why don't you step back here to my office for a minute and we'll talk in private." He led the way around to counter and into a small office in the back.

"Currie is right, you know," as he shut the door on the two of them, putting the saddlebags on the big wooden desk. He took a minute to look through the bags and counted out some money in gold. He turned and held it out to Jack.

"I guess that it isn't much for what you just did for us but I want you to have at least this $500 for a reward. No one but the two of us can ever know for sure about this money I'm giving you. I've known Hank Wilson for many years and I'm his banker and I'm as nervous as that guy who was just talking to you or anyone else in this town that this will not be the end of it. Old man Wilson is a very dangerous man and I don't think that he is going to take this very well at all. If I was to give you some advice it would be to light a shuck out of this town and never look back. Not because you're a coward or anything like that but just because whatever fun you may have been thinking about having in this town is….well

the fun is probably behind you and greener fields lie

elsewhere. If you ride right out of here no one will think

less of you and you'll have this $500 towards a pretty

good time down the road apiece."

Jack had been listening to the speech with

considerable care and he reached out to take the money.

Kind of like blood money, he was thinking, but money's

money so what the hell. Fastest money he'd ever made

and that was for sure. As to the tucking tail twixt his legs

and hurrying down the road, that was a tougher one, but

something was eating on him that Tolliver was probably

right.

Jack had found out a few things about himself that

morning, among them the fact that he could kill armed

bad men as calm and easy as he might a rabbit, and he

really did want to spend a little time thinking things over

before he made any big decisions. There didn't seem to be any doubt in these townsmen's minds that the violent death of the younger Wilson was some sort of a game changer for this town and surely for Jack.

Tolliver continued, "I know this is a lot to digest. Can't really imagine what you are thinking. There you rode into town and took out a couple of bad guys who robbed the bank and shot the sheriff and you are being advised to get out of town as fast as you can. That's pretty crazy but it can get worse. The doctor's murder is proof. That lovely young woman, Lizzy Conan, is the doctor's daughter. The young Wilson was half crazy about her but she wouldn't have a thing to do with him. And besides the fact that he was half drunk first thing this morning that was a good share of the reason that he shot her old man. Neither the girl nor her father had any use at all for the young Wilson or his pa's money, and they didn't care who knew it. I've got to think that it will be a long, long pull for her to recover from what happened here today.

"Well, times a wasting, and I could keep talking all day. I surely do appreciate what you did here today and can't really thank you adequately, but I do hope that you will give what I've been saying considerable and sober thought." The banker was headed for the door.

As they left the office for the customer area of the building Jack cleared his throat and stopped, "I'm thinking about these angles here and would truly like to put go."

The banker grinned and walked Jack to the busted door to point across and down the dusty street. "You've got a few hours, at least. Wilson's spread is a couple of hours away and he will have to bury his son. There'll be a cold beer down at the tavern for you and I will send over to the hotel for a steak and trimmings. It will be over shortly." He turned to Jack and extended his hand, "If you git out of here quick, like I'm hoping, then I may not see you again. I sure do thank you and wish you the best of luck down the trail."

Jack shook and nodded and then stepped for his horse. He removed the reins of the two outlaw 's horses and tied them to the rail. He then walked down towards the bar trailing his horse. There was a lot of stuff roiling around in his mind but he just le things roil for the time being and hitched the horse in front of the bar.

At first it was sort of dark inside but he made out a heavy older fella and a youngish gal behind the bar. He was taking his leisure and she was polishing a glass. There were a trio of wagon drivers down at the far end of the bar having their morning beers. All eyes were on Jack who broke the silence. "Understand a man can get a cold beer in this place."

"That would be right, mister, and the first one's on me," said the barkeep, and he went to draw a beer. "You've only been in this town for an hour or so and you have already put in hell of a day. That was quite a steady piece of shooting you showed us all earlier."

There was a cackle and some loud muttering from down the bar and the barkeep glared in that direction as he set the glass in front of Jack. The woman said something cross but under her breath to the freight haulers and turned towards Jack. "Don't pay no attention to Stretch, there, mister sharpshooter. After a beer or two he considers himself the best shot around and that isn't even to mention that he has been known to keep company with those two roughnecks you just laid out in the street. He could be a bit heartsick on account of that development." and saying that she proceeded to have herself a good belly laugh at the driver's expense.

The biggest of the haulers slammed his mug down and spat. "You shut that gab, Lil, or I'll jerk those knickers up over your ugly head." She laughed even harder despite the bartenders warning grunt but catching his unflinching glare, she coughed a little and went back to polishing the glass with nothing more than a stray giggle.

Jack raised his glass and shrugged before he turned away and walked the length of the barroom to sit alone at a table with his back to the wall. He could see everyone easily from there and he concentrated on the first delicious drink of beer. He figured that the barkeep doubtless wanted to shoot the bull in exchange for the beer but it might be that in this town the less said the better. This did seem to be a very complicated situation that he had got himself into and right now it looked like the best thing to do was to get a good meal into himself and then take the banker's advice and git on down the road.

Thinking about the big hauler over at the bar he reached down and took the string off the hammer of his sidearm. He worked the big gun a little to loosen it and felt like he was getting a case of the nerves over nothing. He mulled over the events of the morning and worked his way through the beer.

Then a young kid was coming through the street door carrying a covered platter up to the bar where he was directed over to Jack. The barkeep followed with a fresh beer and after a few pleasantries departed to let Jack eat. A lift of the cloth revealed a huge steak with fried potatoes and eggs and a mess of beans alongside bread and butter. Jack thought that it might have been the prettiest meal he'd ever set down to and he braced

himself to chew down that much beef. The first bite told

him that this must be from the bankers private stock, the

stuff that the bunkhouse didn't get ahold of. He hardly

had to even chew this meat. This was heavenly! He

worked his way through all of it with occasional sips of

the beer and knew that he had never had a better meal.

Maybe he should give some thought to shooting bad guys

on a regular basis if it was going to mean eating like this

all the time. And no bill, to boot. Now if he could just

have himself a bath and a shave. He found himself

looking over that gal behind the bar. She had quite the

lively figure going on and she sure did seem to be having

a good time, cutting up and laughing all the time. As Jack

was studying her he found her starring right back at him.

He looked away first and was surprised that the image in

his mind was the doctor's daughter from the morning's

doings. Well, now, that was a bit unrealistic for a cowpoke to be wishing for.

At that moment everyone's attention was pulled to the door as a very big man in cowboy gear entered and stood glaring about in the dim light of the barroom. The guy named Stretch stepped forward and nodded pointedly towards where Jack was seated. The big fella got the message and stepped in the general direction of Jack's table, his arms swinging at his sides.

Jack reached down and pulled the pistol to lay it on the table next to his ready hand. Generally that sort of move would be considered a mite unfriendly but the size and demeanor of the giant crossing the room seemed to call for at least that much preparation. This guy was big and he looked like the sort who enjoyed being mean, who wouldn't use a gun unless he had to because he would enjoy it too much doing it with his fists. He was dressed like a cowboy but he didn't carry himself that way but more like an unbeaten prizefighter, with a dangerous menace. He stopped a few feet from Jack's table and smirked down at the pistol.

"You must be the ambushing little prick that killed my friends out there. What, did you stop here to enjoy your last meal?" He spoke in a very low voice that still carried easily and then he started to turn to go. "It won't be today and not tomorrow but soon I'm going to come for you and I promise that I am going to take a long time killing you. So we'll have a lot of time to talk then and get acquainted real good. I reckon that I am going to teach you everything I know about a certain hobby of mine. I got a hard-on just thinking about how good it's going to be." He made a sound then that sounded a little like a giggle, which was a very strange sound coming from that huge, ugly man.

Jack nodded briefly but made no other move. They starred into each other's eyes for a long moment and then the big guy turned and left. The hauler they called Stretch moved away from his fellow drinkers and followed the giant.

The barkeep came over with another beer and starred down at the pistol on the table. "I try to tend to my own business as a general rule but I feel like I should tell you that the chances are that your pistol might not be much use against Grady. I saw him get shot a few years ago and he got the gun away from the shooter and then beat him to death with it. He's meaner than a stomped rattler and he really does enjoy hurting people. He's the foreman out at the W spread and the only man he answers to is old man Wilson. He's a big drinking and whoring buddy of the young Wilson. For your sake, Mister, I hope that you are getting as far as you can from this town as fast as you can. I don't want to hurt your feelings but your life ain't worth a plugged nickel if you stay."

Jack thought it best to keep his own counsel, continuing to say as little as possible. This town and the whole affair seemed to get more complicated all the time. He had shot a bad guy and it was likely going to get him killed, quite soon, maybe today and so maybe it was as good a time as any to take a little trip. Aw hell, it was a strange town anyway. Pretty girls and great steaks but everyone lived in fear of the bunch from the W ranch.

He nodded to the barkeep, polished off the beer and holstered his sidearm. Then, with a neighborly smile for all he headed for the door, mindful that there might well be some nasty surprise or other just outside. He stepped through the door slowly trying to drink in all the sights around him at once. He saw the giant headed out of town on a buckboard that appeared to be loaded with at least one corpse all wrapped up. The mouthy drinker named Stretch was over there watching him go. He then turned and saw Jack on the boardwalk. Jack noticed that Stretch was wearing a pistol now and he wondered if that change might be significant. The tall hauler walked out in the middle of the street and called to Jack.

"That was my friend getting carried out in that wagon, there, and I say that you are a cowardly, ambushing, yeller-bellied son of a bitch. You ain't got the sand to stand right up to a man. You're nothing but a murdering back-shooter." He had got his hand right on the butt of the pistol.

Jack stepped off the boardwalk and away from his horse to face Stretch. He smiled and spoke clearly, "Sticks and stones...Old Stocking," as he raised his left hand, palm up as if welcoming a response. Stretch glared at him and licked his lips thoroughly and raised the hand off the gun butt.

"I wouldn't want to ruin it for Grady and you better believe that I am going to be right there enjoying his work when your last day comes. Soon, Mister, very soon."

Jack tried not to grin. Stretch must be a few beers short of full bucket of courage but that was just fine with the cowboy. He really didn't want to kill this stumblebum. That caused him to wonder just why there was no doubt in his mind that he would have killed the hauler had it come to it. Was it because he was a killer now? Was it because he had noticed that he felt no fear at all in the confrontation with Grady? What he had felt was a calm coldness as though he was completely at ease with his new self. He had always been a better than average shot but that was birds and game. These were other men in his sights now and it didn't seem to bother him at all. That was something to muse about but that would be later and far from this town.

He watched Stretch amble down the street and then he crossed over to what was marked as the general merchandise across from the saloon.

It took Jack no time at all to put together the supplies he needed for a few weeks out on the land plus a couple of extra boxes of ammo. The merchant was very helpful and Jack wasn't surprised that once again there was no charge. It was really tough for him to spend any money in this town. He wondered about the town and it's people and thought that it was not such a good deal to live under the thumb of the powerful rancher, as it appeared that everyone in this town did. He walked across the street with his stuff and loaded it all on the horse. When mounted he took one last long look around the town that had probably changed his life forever and realized that he didn't even know what it was called.

He took the first road he came to towards the north and the open range. As he passed the last of the small houses he saw two women out in front talking. He couldn't help but note that one was the doctor's daughter so he slowed the horse and tugged the brim of his Stetson towards her. He stopped and said softly, "I am so sorry about your loss today, M'am. If there was anything that I could do, you have only to ask." For a second he thought that she was going to respond but then she burst into tears and buried her face in the bosom of the older woman with her. That gal had a less than welcoming look on her face so Jack tugged his hat brim in her direction and turned the horse away towards the open spaces and rode away and out of town. The last thing he saw as he left was a crude little sign by the side of the road. He turned to look at it as he rode by and saw the town was called

Southfork. So, one day was enough in Southfork and he

spurred his horse towards the distant hills.

Jack figured that if he were a wolf he'd be looking

for a moon to howl at as he trotted north. The doc's

daughter had to be the most beautiful woman he'd ever

seen. He had to force his hungry mind away from that

devastating face and figure. It was a difficult struggle but

he persisted because he had to come up with a plan that

had to do with staying alive.

Jack had a pretty good idea that Grady and perhaps

others would make it their priority business to run him to

ground when they had the time and got organized. Jack

figured that he had a day, two at the most before the

pursuit began in earnest. That was the reason that he

headed north. He wasn't going to spend the rest of his

days on the run and he really didn't think that these

buddies of young Wilson were going to make a career out of chasing him down so he had to burn up some of their time. He was figuring to head north for a good piece and then east for a while towards more familiar country before he would turn south and west towards a new life. That was pretty simple but he knew that there would be some adjustments in the days ahead.

He was getting out into the hills now and as he wound through them he suddenly turned and rode up the slope to have a look at his back-trail. Considering how edgy some of his acquaintances had been he was curious if he had someone on his tail. Sure enough there was a lone rider back there about a mile behind him. He looked north and could make out a stand of trees a couple of miles on. Jack turned around down the hill at a good pace and headed for those trees. When he got to the trees he found lots of other cover and a little stream. First a good drink and then he walked the horse across the stream and headed straight north. He rode for a bit and then circled west and back down south to the upper stream. He found a good place to stake out the horse and then looked for a decent spot above the trail to sit a have a look at the following rider.

It was only a short wait before Stretch came into view. He was looking about and taking his time and stopped to dismount for a drink. Jack leveled the rifle and waited for the wagon driver to drink his fill and straighten up before he spoke, " All that beer in the morning makes a fella pretty thirsty, doesn't it. I had a good drink there myself. " Stretch was glued to the spot and every bit of his attention was centered on that rifle barrel pointing right at his belly.

Jack continued, "We didn't really get a chance to finish that conversation we were having in town. Seems like we had only just met, sort of, and you had developed quite a strong opinion of me. My memory is that it wasn't a very positive opinion. Did you want to say more about that or did you get most of all that stuff off your chest back in town where you had an audience?"

Stretch found his voice then. "I don't know who you think you are, mister, pointing that rifle at me and here I am just minding my own business. Whatever was said back in town is water over a dam and over with. Now you had best lower that rifle and let me get on about my business."

"Well, Stretch, ole son, here's what we are going to do instead. You keep that right hand high in the air and undo and drop the gun belt with your left and kick it away. Then take off your shirt, boots and trousers and stack them nice right there by the stump."

The big hauler hesitated in the unbuckling as he digested what Jack had said. He looked like he had something to say as he starred at the rifle.

"You can undo that gunbelt and drop it or you can try you luck. That will be your call, "Jack said with soft menace.

The gunbelt hit the ground and Stretch stripped to his long johns. Jack studied that look for a moment and then decided. "Take them off, too. Now tie your shirt around your waist and put those boots back on. It's a long walk back to town." He waited, patiently as Stretch glared and followed directions and then continued in a hard voice. "You still have your life, fella, which is more than you'd have left me, and after your nice walk back to town this afternoon perhaps you might give some thought to picking out a better grade of friends .Now you get moving and if you do turn around I'm going to put a round right in that fat ass of yours. Now move!"

Jack watched Stretch hobble away holding onto his covering shirt .He almost laughed out loud but thought better of it.

He was tired of this freight hauler and he was almost kicking himself that he was a fool to make this kind of an enemy and leave him alive. Jack wasn't a murderer but this was very bad business to leave a back trail like this. It was difficult to ignore the fact that his new life was getting so complicated and it had only just begun a few hours ago. Jack had plenty to think about as he watched till Stretch was almost out of sight. He gathered up Stretch's stuff and secured it to his mount before leading the animal back through the woods to where he had tethered his own horse.

Jack crossed the creek again and continued north, traveling steadily for another couple of hours. Then he pulled up and dismounted for a stretch. He tethered his mount and then led the hauler's horse for a ways down the back trail and let it loose towards town with a good smack on the backside.

Shortly thereafter Jack found what he thought was a pretty good spot at another small stream and he rode, picking his way carefully down the middle of a shallow stream for a couple of miles to slow down any pursuers. Since it was coming on evening he left the stream and moved off in an easterly direction through the hills till he found a nice secluded spot to camp for the night. Jack was no stranger to the wilderness but he figured that his survival skills could use a little honing as he traveled mostly east and then in a southerly direction. He didn't feel like he had to be in a big rush. If he found a spot where there was good cover, a good view, game, and water he could always throw up a lean-to and stay a couple of days.

He stayed to the higher ground as he headed south keeping a very close eye on his back trail and all points of the compass to avoid contact as much as possible. It was slower going keeping to the higher ground but it did make it easier to avoid a couple of sizable settlements. Slow didn't seem that bad right now, anyway, as Jack tried to sort out his options for the near future. So, leave very little in the way of tracks, keep moving and stay alive. There was plenty of game about for fresh meat and plenty of time for practice with the firearms.

PART II

Wakefield

A pleasant few weeks passed in this fashion. One morning, having risen early, Jack was taking a minute with a smoke near the top of a hill over looking a river valley. He had been following the river for some days now and stayed just out of sight of the road that followed the watercourse. He heard a commotion down in the general direction of the road and dismounted to crawl up to the top of the hillock and have a look. There was a stage tearing along the road, the driver cracking the whip from time to time. That was what he'd heard and he watched as the stage moved along right below him.

Quite suddenly three riders broke from the river trees and bore down on the coach with pistols raised and firing. They really had the drop on the stagehands and the fellow riding shotgun went down and off the stage immediately. He rolled in the dust and lay still as the gunmen concentrated on the driver. He was hit a couple of times and fell forward as one gunman grabbed the right side lead horse and the stagecoach came to a halt in short order. It had all happened very quickly and now the door of the stage was being opened and the passengers were getting out.

From where Jack was watching it appeared like they stage occupants comprised an older couple and a flashily dressed guy like a drummer or something of that sort. Jack saw them handing over stuff to the robbers and he was trying to think what he should or wanted to do. Jack had found out recently that interfering with a robbery in progress could lead to a lot of unintended consequences. He didn't kid himself that he could do anything anyway from this position and distance. There would be plenty of chance when the bad guys left to go down and lend a hand, if he so chose.

At that moment the robbers were backing away when one stopped and shot all of the passengers. He shot them all dead while Jack watched in amazement. Jack rolled over on his back and gazed at the bright blue sky. He thought about his rifle but discarded the idea…he couldn't get them all anyway. As his shock and rage cooled Jack considered that there might be a better way to intervene in this affair.

Life out on the range was an endless lesson in the importance of the virtue of patience, and Jack had learned to be a very patient man, as needed. From his distant vantage point Jack watched the robbers pack the strongbox and some other stuff on a coach horse and head off the road into the hills well to the west. Jack moved out smartly and had little problem picking up the trail of the bandits. He moved on with some caution until he spotted them winding through the hills. He adjusted his pace accordingly to keep them in sight. They traveled generally west into the hills but stayed mostly in the wooded areas. They were making pretty good time and then suddenly stopped. They dismounted while Jack pulled up a third of a mile behind them.

Jack figured it was way early to camp but also that these robbers would have no fear of early pursuit. Killing everyone could well lead to a more relaxed escape. He heard a gunshot and then shortly they were mounted and moving again. Jack followed and came upon the broken strongbox and an empty whiskey bottle. Jack took that empty bottle as a good sign. He was hoping that the lads were in a real party mood after their exploits back on the coach road. He moved off along their trail and the day wore on into evening. It would be a lot dicier to follow after dark so Jack was relieved when they stopped and then got about making camp.

Jack retraced his steps a quarter mile, staked his horse and made a cold camp. He waited for a couple of hours before he began to make his way back to the outlaw camp. Shortly he found them with the help of their fire and snoring. The fellow doing sentry duty was not hard to spot and Jack settled down to wait for his opportunity. After about an hour and a lot more pulls from the bottle the sentry slumped over in sleep.

Jack had his rifle with him for a little extra firepower and he sat for another hour going over his options. The fire was very low and there was very little light from the moon so it was quite dark there in the woods. Jack was thinking that the sentry duty would likely be shared and so he waited. Sure enough and half an hour later and one of the prone sleepers moved around and rose and after throwing more wood on the fire strode over to the sentry who had passed out. He cursed him loudly and gave him a mighty kick in the side whereupon the fellow yelled in pain and rolled away from that boot. The relief sentry cursed again and then turned to put more wood on the fire. He then dug out some makings and started rolling a smoke. The first sentry groused audibly for a while and then rolled over and went to sleep, noisily. Jack watched, waiting patiently.

The new sentry tended the fire and smoked and more time passed. Jack knew that it wouldn't get much better than it was right then. He found a fist sized rock at his feet and crawled even closer the cam, staying very low to the ground. The crackle of the fire was a nice background as Jack moved to what seemed a pretty good place. He then hefted the rock over the outlaws to the woods beyond and there was a satisfying racket to seize the sentry's attention. He swung to the sound with his gun extended and moved to the side in case he was a target. Jack gave a low cough and the outlaw was getting himself turned around again when Jack shot him twice and turned on the sleepers. The guy by the fire was just trying to sit up when Jack put a round into the middle of his chest. The first sentry was making a mighty effort to get his gun out when Jack fired again, another two rounds.

It was suddenly very quiet and Jack holstered his pistol and walked over to his targets. He prodded each with the rifle, confirming that all were dead, noting that the fellow who had slept straight through was left handed. He pulled the belt off the dead outlaw and buckled it on himself. The revolver was quite new and Jack liked the feel of it. He squeezed off a few rounds with his left hand and felt okay about it. Might have to put in some time with that later. Then he went back for his horse and gear. He took care of the horse and after a final check around he laid down for what remained of the night.

Jack rose at dawn and after a quick breakfast started to clean up the camp. Loading the dead robbers on their mounts and securing them for the journey was a lot of work but it was also quite satisfying. When all was loaded and tied down tight Jack headed his string of horses in the general direction of the road. He figured there must be a town fairly close, the town that the stage had failed to make. After a few hours he saw the coach road from the top of a hill and noticed a single rider approaching it from out of the hills up ahead. The horseman reached the road, heading west at a brisk trot. Curious about the rider's origin, Jack decided to retrace the rider's path. Jack made his way down to the road and stayed with it to the rider's entry point. He left the stage road and followed a well worn trail around the base of a hill with his string trailing along behind.

Shortly he saw a small farmstead ahead with a well out front and he rode slowly towards the house. He was almost to the well when the door of the house opened and a woman in a straw hat and a shapeless brown dress emerged. She held a rifle pointed right at him, which prompted Jack to rein in and lift his hands slowly.

"Pardon me Ma'am," he yelled, "but I just wanted to get a drink. I don't want to make any trouble for you. Just a quick drink for me and these horses and I'll be on my way."

The rifle stayed steady on him but she did nod towards the water. She spoke in a loud and clear voice. "I want you to know that I am a pretty decent shot with this thing and when I shoot I always shoot to kill. Get your drink and then get off down the road with ya. I don't like the looks of you and I really don't like the looks of your companions." She rested the barrel on the top of a post and followed Jack's every move.

"Well, shucks, Ma'am, I reckon I'm not much to look at in the best of times. These riding buddies of mine are headed for their final resting place, en route, I would think, to the hell that they have coming to them. They robbed a coach back down the road apiece yesterday and shot the crew and the passengers in as cold a fashion as you ever laid eyes on. Guess, at that, they won't be needing a drink, not any more." Upon saying that, Jack had a good laugh at his own wit.

The gal with the rifle studied him with unblinking eyes, so Jack left off his mirth and got to the horses. He heard a stick break and turned to find the woman right behind him with the rifle still pointed but now looking closer at the outlaws bodies. She shifted her eyes back to Jack and backed away a step. She looked to be around twenty and Jack was stunned to see how attractive she was. The flashing eyes, the long black curly hair, up close she was breathtaking.

"So, who shot all these bad guys, anyway? I hope that you aren't going to tell me that you shot down all these guys by yourself and now you're delivering them to the undertaker. In the first place, why didn't you just leave them where you found them? In the second place, you could really use a bath." She paused and glared at him.

Jack didn't trust himself to say a word. He tossed off his hat threw some water on his face. He managed a big grin for her and then went back to watering the horses. He then reached for his hat but at the corner of his vision he saw the rifle waving back and forth. He looked up to see her shaking her head at him and the hat.

"Leave that dirty old thing there and wash up a lot better than that. Maybe I'll rustle up a little lunch for you before you take off to the undertaker's." She turned and strode purposefully towards the house. She stopped right then and turned. "You never did get around to saying who shot all those bad guys," she said. "Are you just that modest or is it that you can't remember?" She waited there for a minute for his reply but Jack just smiled at her and pulled off his shirt to get washed for lunch. She watched and then continued to the house, shaking her head.

Jack cleaned up and then went in to eat. It seemed like a good spell since breakfast, and he ate with gusto and frequent praise for the cook. She mostly just stood there watching him work through the food and smiling at the compliments. He had noticed that her shirt was unbuttoned down far enough for him to see the swell of her breasts. When he did look up Jack's eyes went right to the cleavage between those breasts. It was making him feel kind of dizzy so he tried to look away.

"They don't go with the lunch," she said sternly, "necessarily." Her eyes were anything but stern and she walked towards him as she undid one more button and then another button on her dress. Another step and another button and now Jack's face was buried in her cleavage. She smelled of flowers, he thought maybe lilac.

Jack moved to look up at her and she flicked the straps from her shoulders and the dress floated down to the floor. Her charms revealed, she purred softly as she gathered him closer and whispered, "I'm going to turn nineteen next week and I think that you must be my early birthday present." Jack didn't reply because he felt, as he swept her up and carried her to the feather bed, like he might well be going to heaven. They went there together and then again and then lay there in each other's arms for a while, completely spent. Finally Jack forced himself away from her and started dressing to go.

"You know, Ma'am, this just might be the best lunch I've ever had," he said as he looked down at her naked body. He couldn't resist one last kiss and then he pulled on his boots and headed for the door. She stretched noisily and got up to follow him.

She yawned and slapped him on the bottom. "Drop by whenever you're in the area but be sure that my old man is off to town. I don't think that he would approve of our new friendship." They had a good laugh and a last kiss, and Jack was out the door. He mounted and was leading his string out when he turned in the saddle for a last look. She was standing in front of the cabin, buck naked, waving goodbye with the rifle butt resting on her hip. She made a very fetching picture, a memory to treasure. Jack waved back with a wide grin and turned back to the trail to return to the coach road.

There was plenty to muse about these days, not the least of which being how different his life was. He wondered if he was becoming a whole different fellow in the process. The cowboy who had ridden into the middle of a bank robbery a few weeks back seemed very distant now, very distant indeed.

After about an hour he met a single rider coming the other way. He was an older fellow with a serious set to his jaw. He nodded but said nothing as they met. Then he stopped and starred as Jack nodded in return and filed past with his funeral string in tow.

Jack wondered if he would ever be back this way; ever see her again. Was she really attracted to him or to a ruthless gunman or was there a difference? He remembered the group trussed up behind him and gave a little shudder. No matter why it had come about, and no matter how pleasant, she was a married woman. Funny, when he thought about it, that they didn't even know each other's names, she and him, but she would be hard to forget.

Another hour and he saw a sign for the town of Wakefield, pop: 422. Riding into town and down the main street gave him a feeling of being on parade. He kept his eyes to the front but out of the corners of his vision it was obvious that the town was coming to a stop as he rode along. People stopped and gawked and others came out of doorways and joined the impromptu audience. Jack saw a small building with a "City Jail" sign decorating it so he rode right up to the front door. An older, well fed fella with a great mustache and wearing a tin star slouched in his shaded chair next to the door. He and Jack regarded each other for a long moment. Jack broke the silence. "I wonder if I have the honor of addressing the sheriff of this town," he said.

"I don't know what the hell honor has to do with it but you've got yourself quite a following there," the man replied. "I know you are going to have a good explanation for all those horses. The one with the marks of a stage horse is of particular interest."

Jack dismounted and tethered his horse before he turned to the sheriff. "It isn't a long story I'll be boring you with, sheriff. My name is Jack McGill. Yesterday from a hill well above I saw these fellows break cover and attack the stagecoach headed this way. They shot the guard and driver and stopped the stage. They then got the passengers out and robbed them. Then they shot all of them, loaded the strongbox on the stage hoss and hightailed it into the hills up ahead of my position. I followed them and surprised them and here we are." Jack walked over to the stage horse to grab the saddlebags on it and bring them over to drape them over the hitch rail. "I believe that you will find the money from the strongbox in these bags. I didn't disturb it."

The old sheriff looked at Jack very cynically. He pushed a nasty looking cigar in his lips and took his time lighting it before he pushed himself to his feet and stepped off the boardwalk to glance into the saddlebags. He moved around Jack to look at the corpses, taking a good deal of time in doing so. A considerable crowd had gathered and was pushing up pretty close. The lawman spread his arms wide in a gesture to persuade the populace to stay back and then walked back to Jack.

He spoke with considerable sarcasm. "It appears that what we have here is a very accomplished do-gooder. All these fellas were shot in the front, which is interesting because they must have been armed from the looks of all these guns. So, that means that you must be quite the pistolero. But if that's the case then how come I've never heard of you? And if you are that goddamned good then why didn't you just go ahead and save the passengers, at least?"

"Sheriff, I'm just a cowboy between jobs, not a gunslinger. And there was nothing to do during the robbery as it happened too fast and I was way out of effective range for that much rifle work. And…just so you don't get the wrong impression of me, I might as well ask if there is a reward for returning this money. I could use a new set of clothes." Jack finished with the hint of a grin.

The sheriff glared at him and walked past him across the boardwalk and into the jail. He came right back out with a handful of wanted posters and stopped to address the crowd. "All you folks can go about your business now. There is no more excitement or drama here. This young fellow has stolen all of the drama from this moment. So, lets break it up let me go about my work here." He threw the saddlebags of loot over his shoulder and said in a lower voice to Jack, "Who do you think these fellas are, McGill? Aren't you the least bit interested in who you gun down? In this case it might be worth quite a bit of money to you to establish their identities. There's just a chance these old posters will be helpful.

"Just to fill you in on what's happened at this end, you might be surprised to learn that the shotgun guard survived the attack and is over at the doc's right now. I was hoping to talk to him some more before I put together a posse to go after these killers. They already had a day on us and it would be nice to find out anything useful. Also, the stage line has a detective headed this way and he should be here in town any time. Since you're here with the money and the dead outlaws looks like we've got a complete change of plans. Lets take these horses over to the undertaker's place and get these guys down so we can look at them."

He took the lead for the trailing horses and led the way up the street with a smaller crowd, mostly kids, in dogged pursuit. Jack was thinking that he and that crotchety old sheriff were practically fast friends now. But it was true that the old lawdog could stay there in his chair all afternoon rather than riding off to hell and gone with his posse.

They set off to see the carpenter's shop with a quick stop at the hotel to drop off the money to be held in the safe. There were also some personal valuables of the murdered passengers to examine but the sheriff just left all that with the money. He negotiated a county payment with the undertaker and they pushed the bodies off the horses to give the faces a better look. The sheriff passed the wanted posters around and the speculation commenced. There were a couple of good possibilities.

Shortly a hard looking fella rode up and introduced himself as Elmer Jones, stage detective. He dismounted and turned to the bodies, then the posters and again at the bodies and said, "It's like I was thinking. It's the Durban boys and their cousin Pallen. They have hit us before down by Readesville. They were a bad bunch that just got more vicious. It's still kind of a shock that they killed those passengers in cold blood. Someone said that the guard was still alive."

The sheriff nodded and said, "I don't know if he is going to make it but he was able to tell us that he thought there were three of them that attacked the stage." The detective turned to Jack for his tale, which the cowboy told briefly.

Jones was studying Jack with considerable interest. "You can tell me more if you want, but later. I will tell you that return of the strongbox contents is worth $500. These fellas, living or in their current condition are worth $1800, so if you want to walk over to the bank with me I can get you your money. Then maybe you can buy the sheriff and I a cold beer. While we're walking you can maybe tell me how you single handedly bested this bunch and there isn't a mark on you."

"Well," said Jack humbly, "they may have been a little sleepy and distracted at their last moment. They may well have done better if I had given them more time to compose themselves."

Jones laughed and clapped Jack on the shoulder. "Maybe I'll buy you a beer," he said. The business at the bank was quick and then they headed for the saloon. The first round of beers was on the house and the crowd was growing again. Jack said as little as possible, stayed for a couple of rounds and took off to the hotel for a bath. On the way he picked up some new clothes and stopped at the shoemakers to order a new pair of boots and a money belt. He got a room and a bath and shave and in the new duds he felt like a new man.

After a quick nap Jack went down to the dining room for the biggest steak on the menu washed down with a couple of beers. No one approached him while he ate but he couldn't shake the feeling that everybody in the room was staring at him. Whenever he looked up from his plate people nodded and looked away. It was uncomfortable and Jack had a hunch he wouldn't learn to like it.

It had been a short night and a long day and a good night's sleep was sounding pretty good. Jack secured his money in the hotel safe and purchased a bottle of whiskey. With that and a jug of water he headed for his room. He braced the door closed and dragged a chair over to the window to look down on main street, staying back out of sight from those from down below. He poured himself some whiskey and had a long pull on the water jug to chase it down.

There was a lot to think about. He didn't want to be too paranoid but all this attention was new and very uncomfortable. He didn't like it a bit. He had a lot of money now and with the attention he felt like a target, but he had no idea who his enemies were. He had always been a loner, but right now he thought it might not be so bad to have a friend. Probably the first thing he ought to do was to get out of this town.

Jack decided it was high time to develop a plan for his life. He had a lot of money now, more than he had ever dreamed of having at one time. He really didn't want to go on a tear with the girls and the booze until he was broke again. He was thinking about settling down with a good woman, finding their own place and raising some cattle and horses. That had a nice sound to it but he would need more money and a good woman, one who wasn't already spoken for.

Whenever he was worrying over the direction of his life these days his thoughts would eventually wander back to Lizzy Conan, the beauty from the Southfork bank

He found it hard to believe that she would ever have anything to do with him, a cowboy turned gunslinger. But a fellow did need a dream to hang onto, and she was surely the stuff of dreams. He sat there for quite a spell looking down on the activity in the street below and letting his thoughts wander over the past and into the future. Finally he took care of business, checked the door and hit the sack.

Jack was up early and he headed down to the dining room for breakfast. The smell of coffee was wonderful, bracing. The sheriff and the stage detective were settling in for breakfast and motioned him over to join them. Jack grabbed a cup of coffee and sat down with them.

The sheriff spoke first. "Early to bed and up early. All that gun fighting must have plumb wore you out. A lot of yahoos sitting on that kind of money would have hit the whiskey and whores full speed and woke up in a week. Might as well tell you that I noticed a pistol and gun belt missing, or was I wrong there?"

Jack grinned ruefully and said, "No, sheriff, you're right about that. I neglected to mention that and would like to make it right with you. What do I owe you for the additional firepower?"

The sheriff waved the thought away and shrugged. "A cowpuncher-bounty hunter that needs more fire power? Sounds like a fella who is hanging up his lasso for the time being. Jones here," motioning to the detective, "who goes by the name of Elmer, is looking for a good man with your sort of appreciation for firepower." He nodded to Jones.

"As a matter of fact," the stage detective said, "I am looking for an intelligent, honest gunslinger. I had no idea that such a fella existed. You pull off a stunt like you did with those stage robbers all on your own notion and alone and you've got a piss pot full of money and instead of taking on all the whiskey and women in town you go off and get a good night's sleep. You might well be one of a kind."

Jack thought it over and said, "It had been a long day and I'm not really used to attention. I spent most of the last ten years sleeping under the stars or in some way off line shack. Really not all that used to people and certainly not used to this kind of scrutiny. And that money makes me feel like a target. Reckon that it is time to move on. So, tell me why you're looking for a boring gunhand."

"I didn't say boring and doubt you would be called that. I could use a good hand for maybe a month or so. The stage line is having some difficulties over west of Longstreet, which is about sixty or so miles west of here.

There's a gang that hangs out back in those foothills and likes to hit a train now and again. Once in a while for a change of pace they will knock off a stage. They have hit us twice and my next assignment is to travel out that way and see if I can find any sign of them. They have had some pretty decent hauls in the last year so they don't strike real regular.

"If you're in between jobs I would be willing to put you on the payroll. It pays three times cowpuncher wages, and we split any bounties or rewards. I'm leaving before noon. I have to see to that shot-up guard and then get some provisions together. What do you think?"

Jack thought about his life-plan and wondered if this might not be the next step. He extended his hand to Elmer to shake on it and they finished breakfast. The three of them then set off to look in on the stage guard at the doc's office. The guard looked like the devil, but he was conscious and awake. He had been filled in on the rest of the story. Jack found his gruff gratitude a little embarrassing but the guard and the dead driver went back a long ways and were old friends. The guard was quite tickled that his friend had been so quickly revenged. He squeezed Jack's hand with real emotion.

That visit behind them, Elmer and Jack left the sheriff and headed for the mercantile to stock up for the road. The detective said, "I heard a story lately about some cowboy who stumbled into a bank robbery way up north of here and he shot the two outlaws out of their saddles as they tried to run him down, pouring lead at him. Quite the cool customer that cowpuncher was, or at least that was the way the story went. I don't suppose that any of that rings a bell with you, Jack."

Jack just grinned for an answer and right then a young fellow ran right into him knocking him back and almost off balance. Jack steadied himself and turned to the youngster who was dressed shabbily but sporting a sidearm. He was seething and squaring off on Jack.

"You goddamned clumsy son of a bitch!" The kid was yelling. "You run right into me like you own the street. Well now, if it ain't that ambushing bounty hunter. I'm going to hear an apology right now or I am going to put you down right here in the street like the yellow cur you are!" The fingers of his right hand were twitching in the neighborhood of his sidearm. He was trying his best to look braced and ready.

Jack kept his hands well up and approached the youngster slowly as people hurried to get out of the line of fire. Jack said in a loud voice, "I am so sorry about that collision. And it was all my fault as I was talking to my friend here about hardtack and some such. It was very rude of me, and I apologize from the bottom of my heart!" Jack was moving as he talked and was now almost nose to nose with the young ruffian, who shook his head in a violent negative. Jack stuck out his mitt as though to shake hands. The enraged youngster was jerking the gun from the holster when Jack kicked him in the crotch as hard as he could. Jack's left hand snaked out to hold the gun down and he redirected his right fist to the point of the kid's jaw. It was a beautiful shot and he heard a satisfying crack as the kid's eyes rolled back and he collapsed in a heap, dropping the side arm. Jack bent to pick it up and straightened to look around.

"This fella have any friends hereabouts?" No one responded so Jack continued, "I am going to leave this gun with the storekeeper for when the lad comes out of it. If he does have a friend here who is just being shy, maybe you could try to talk a little sense into him about keeping the proper distance from his target." Jack turned back towards the store and almost ran into the old sheriff.

The lawman grunted and reached for the pistol. "Well, I guess that you were right about the attention problem. I do think that you are going to have to work at getting along a little better with others. Not with this little asshole, though; tell ya, that boy ain't worth shooting. He's always looking for trouble and he is the kind who is going to be looking for your back, if you know what I mean. In this case, if you had shot him you'd have saved the town a lot of future problems." The sheriff studied Jack for a second and then said, " You are an interesting fellow, McGill. Probably good that you are headed down the road but look in if you ever come back this way." He stuck out his mitt, adding, "The town remains in your debt."

Jack rejoined Elmer and they continued towards the store. Elmer said thoughtfully, " That was a decent thing you done, no question, but you won't get away with that again. You are getting to be a guy with a legend behind your name, Jack, and that legend will be tough to shake. Time to get out on the open road and put some distance between you and the fellas that are bound to come looking for you." Jack nodded thoughtfully as they entered the store.

They purchased bacon, beans, whiskey, flour and ammo for the trip. Elmer negotiated with the sheriff for the best of the outlaw horses for use as a pack animal. He gave Elmer a good deal. They then made stops at the shoemaker for Jack's boots and at the hotel where Jack retrieved his money and packed it into his new money belt. They had a couple of beers and bought a bunch of sandwiches for the road and then headed out of town as quietly as possible. Shortly the road forked and they

headed west.

Part III

Longstreet

They moved steadily and Elmer noted that Jack always kept an eye on the back trail. The second day he mentioned it and Jack told him briefly about Southfork and afterwards. The detective was thoughtful. "It isn't a bad habit to have and will likely come in handy in the weeks ahead."

Much of the trip they rode in silence but Elmer did tell Jack about some of his adventures with the stage company. His history before that was a little hazy but Jack didn't press him to fill in everything. Probably most people had some skeletons in the back room and Jack was prepared to trust this guy. He had never seen him under pressure but thought he could probably handle himself.

They reached Longstreet on the third day and got rooms for the night. It was just another dusty little western town of no particular accomplishment. Elmer felt it would suit them nicely as a base of operations while in pursuit of the outlaws. Jack parked his money belt in the hotel safe and the pair of them headed out for a few beers after arranging for fried chicken and trimmings to be sent along to the saloon.

They sat at the bar and ordered beers to wash out the dust of the trail. The bar maid was kind of cute and she flirted a little before moving down the bar. Elmer took the opportunity to inquire. "So, tell me if you feel like it, about that affair up in Southfork. What caused you to get involved in a thing like that? What were you thinking, putting your life at risk in goings on that was none of your affair?"

Jack scratched the back of his head and took his time answering. "I'm not sure that I know the answer to that although I've spent a passel of time thinking about it during the last few weeks. In Southfork I think that it was seeing those fellas gun down the sheriff and laughing about it. That pissed me off. Out on the stage road it maybe was watching the robbers gun down the passengers. I think that what I felt both times that if I was the victim or a relative I might be glad that a stranger saw something wrong or as just pure bullshit and the stranger just set things right…like the stranger just stepped in and balanced the books, at least a little. Does that make any sense to you? You seem like a fella who has kicked around a good deal and maybe seen some darker days. It is sort of like you could watch and then get out of the way and let it go down or you could follow your gut and take a stand right there." He paused for a drink and when Elmer said nothing immediately, Jack looked down and lowered his voice a little, "Also, not sure just why but killing those guys was easy. I don't mean out shooting them because I've always been a pretty good shot. Also, I had plenty of time to do it the smart way and it never entered my mind that I would lose. I'm talking about the killing of those guys, and I'd never killed a man before. Well, killing them meant nothing. I really just executed them and I have never had any second thoughts about it. It's as though they deserved killing and I was right there to carry out the sentence. End of story." Jack looked up with a smile and realized the barmaid was standing right there. The look on her face was deadpan, but he knew she'd been listening. He winked and ordered more beer. Jack glanced at Elmer who seemed lost in thought.

The beers arrived and Jack smiled and winked at the gal again when he sensed someone behind him as a throat was cleared. Jack and Elmer turned at the same time to find a big fellow standing right behind them and holding his empty beer mug upside down. He said in a strained voice, "Hey, Sally, what's a guy gotta do to get a drink around here? Seems like you're spending all your time jawing down at this end of the bar."

She pushed both palms towards the big guy and shook her head in a curt negative. "Earl, you're drinking too fast and you know we'll have no trouble here. I'm on the way down to your place with a fresh beer." She was out of Jack and Elmer's vision, but the big fella backed away as she motioned abruptly towards the other end of the bar.

"What the devil was that all about, do you think," asked Jack?

Elmer had a gulp of beer before answering, "I think that the little gal didn't want her friend to be messing around with folks that talk that easy about killing. I gotta tell you that I don't know the answers to your questions. I've done some killing and know that it is a hard thing, harder on some than on others in the doing of it. I'm going to tell you what I think, for sure. From what I've seen of you and what you're capable of, I'm glad you're on my side, especially in the kind of work that we may be called upon to do in these days ahead. For some reason you turned in the money when nobody even knew you had it. That makes you more honest than most of the lawmen you'll run across. I'd say that ole Bob Curry, the sheriff back in Wakefield, is a pretty good man but most of the lawdogs you deal with seem like they could operate on either side of the law, depending on the time of day." He stopped to stare into his beer and then had a long pull on it.

Jack waited for a minute and then asked what he thought was the obvious question. "What about you? Seems like we've established that I am an incurable do-gooder. What's your take on all this right and wrong stuff?"

Elmer shrugged heavily and said, "I've seen a bunch of life, including a bit of the war and after. I've used a gun and hired out my gun before I ended up doing this. I didn't much care for the bad guy business and I sort of like going after those bastards. Guess that I'm a pretty hard fella and I don't mind shooting them or locking them up if it comes to that. It's a job but it's a little better than that, if you get my drift." He gave Jack a lopsided grin and ordered a couple more beers as the chicken arrived. They chowed down and hung around for another round and then called it a night.

After a big breakfast the next morning they went by the sheriff's office. Elmer had worked in the area before and knew and liked the lawman. He introduced Jack with little background, just that Jack was a man to be trusted. He then told the sheriff that they were going to ride out in search of the Weaver gang. The sheriff was all ears and offered to be of whatever assistance he could.

The train gang had been around for a long time and had even pulled some jobs close to his jurisdiction. As for news or good information on the gang the sheriff didn't really have much that was current except the usual intelligence that the gang was well armed, well led and apparently very disciplined. Rumor had it that a pair of brothers named Cyrus and Paul Weaver led the gang and did all the thinking. They had done some killing but had never lost a man. The planning and execution of their robberies was considered flawless.

The sheriff did point out that Elmer and Jack were traveling pretty light against long odds. "Hell, if I was going out after this bunch think that I would load up a bit. I'd take eight or ten good men and I believe that I'd take a few sticks of dynamite. You might consider borrowing that old double barrel ten gauge over in the corner. It's got short barrels and a pistol grip and I can tell you when you touch it off it's more like a cannon than a shotgun."

Jack walked over and hefted the old gun. He thumbed the lever over to break it open and looked down the barrel. He checked the triggers and hammers and snapped it shut. He grinned in spite of himself at what a devilishly uncomplicated machine it was, so simple and so deadly.

"Think that I'll take you up on your offer, sheriff. If Elmer and I have to put a lot of lead in the air of a sudden, this thing full of double ought might be just the ticket."

Elmer rose and smiled, "That's not bad advice, sheriff. We will grab a few sticks of dynamite but other than that I want to travel pretty light this time and really study the lay of the land out there. I really don't have any thought about taking this gang on with just the two of us. We're going to look for sign and try to stay clear of trouble. If we can find anything of interest then I'll take it to the stage company and we'll decide how to proceed. We don't know the truth yet but my guess right now is that you'd need a good sized posse to go after this gang and get the job done."

The sheriff shrugged as he stood to see them off. "I like the idea of not taking any chances. If you run into this bunch try to get clear and then try to get the hell out of those hills, pronto." Jack and Elmer didn't argue with him. They shook hands with the old lawman and headed for the general merchandize to get ready for the road. Jack pushed the ten gauge inside his cartridge belt and it didn't feel that bad. He did get a chuckle out of Elmer.

Jack's first purchase at the store was a long strip of hide to hang the ten gauge off his shoulder behind his left arm. They picked up ten sticks of fused dynamite, a box of double-ought for the scattergun and a box of cheap cigars that Elmer had a weakness for. Jack got to studying a smaller revolver, a thirty-two gauge, and he asked the clerk for a closer look. He liked the feel of it, and hiking up his trouser leg he checked to make sure it would fit his boot top. Finding that it did, he grabbed a cutter and clipped a length of heavy wire. He twisted it into a clip holster, and after loading the small revolver he clipped it on the inside of his right boot. Covered by his pant leg the gun disappeared. Elmer was getting quite a kick out of his preparations. They made a final check of gear and provisions and took the road to the west and into the hills.

They traveled till late and finally camped in a small grove of trees by a stream. Sitting around the campfire, Elmer set out a rough outline of his plan. "It's about another twenty miles to the place where the attempted stage holdup took place. I want to move around in the high country on both sides of the road there with an eye towards finding good vantage points from which to study the road. These fellas had to have a man up high keeping an eye on the road, a member of the gang who could warn them of possible problems such as those guarded cargo wagons that broke up the stage robbery. That shows more discipline and planning than you would usually expect from stage robbers. I would have to guess that the work they have done with trains has schooled them a bit for other endeavors."

He puffed on his cigar and worried the fire with a stick. "I doubt that their main camp is near here but would bet that they know these hills real good. We are at a considerable disadvantage, but that is one more reason that I want to check out some of the high spots to get a better idea of the lay of the land. I'll take first watch if you want to get some shut eye."

Jack stretched and made a place to lie down. He kept his ten gauge and the saddlebag with the cigars and dynamite right close. He slept and dreamt about the voluptuous farm wife and having lunch with her again. When Elmer woke him for a spell at sentry he kept right on thinking about her. He wondered if he would ever see her again but he really didn't see that happening. Well, she would always be a great memory, waving goodbye without a stitch and her rifle at the ready.

They moved steadily west for another day and camped well away from the road to the north. They spent the next couple of days combing the higher elevations above and along a ten-mile section of road but never saw much that interested Elmer. They broke camp the following morning and headed south where they continued the search. They not only were not finding the good vantage spots they expected but also very little sign of travelers. On the afternoon of the fifth day they stumbled on a better-used track coming generally from the west and south. Following it towards the stage road, they ran into a cutaway up around and to the top of a high bluff. As they emerged into the open at the top Elmer's mug split into a big grin. Well below and through the hills they could see three pretty good chunks of the stage road. This was a perfect lookout post for fellas with a little larceny in their hearts.

The weather was changing. It was looking like a good chance of a storm so after a further look around they started down the trail in search of a little shelter from the elements. Looking up they could see the storm roaring down on them out of the mountains. Upon arrival at the lower trail they retraced their steps towards a cliff edge they'd spotted earlier that would afford them some shelter from the storm. The wind was quickening and the rain was starting to pelt them. Jack was leading slightly, bending into the wind as they rode wide around a broken rock face.

Suddenly, and less than twenty feet away, there appeared a group of mounted men riding towards them all bunched together along the trail. Jack reached his left hand back to the pistol grip of the shotgun and pushed it forward while his right hand wrapped around the barrels to level it. No one else moved for a long second as each man tried to come to some decision about how to proceed. Jack didn't know for sure who these riders were but there did seem to be a pretty good chance of trouble as he pulled back both hammers. Elmer was just behind and to his right.

The second rider made his move for his pistol when Jack rose up in the stirrups and the rain and pulled both triggers. The first two riders went down with one of the horses and the third rider was hit and reeling. The empty horse stumbled backward and Jack's mount slewed to the left as Jack dropped the shotgun and reached for his forty-five. Elmer was emptying his pistol at the fourth and fifth riders. The third rider, slowed by the buckshot, was bringing up his pistol when Jack fired three times. The third rider dropped the pistol and slumped to the side. The fifth and last rider was spurring away back down the trail and lost to the storm. Jack thought he might have been hit but visibility was poor in the driving rain and one really couldn't be sure.

Elmer and Jack urged their horses forward for a better look, keeping their side arms at the ready. Jack dismounted while

Elmer took his reins and kept watch. Jack checked their handiwork and grabbed the horses' reins as he went. All four riders were quite dead. Jack was glad to see that the fallen horse was struggling to get up, and then did with apparently nothing worse than a jagged crease on the top of its head, doubtless from the buckshot. Jack grabbed the reins while he kept his distance, guessing that the mare might be a little moody. He turned to Elmer and raised both palms with two sets of reins in each and managed a crooked grin in the pouring rain.

Elmer regarded him from under his hat brim. "Well, guess you'd have to say that the shotgun did come in handy. Of course it does make quite a difference who has it in hand." He was just shaking his head at the turn of events. This young cowboy was quite a piece of work in a fight.

"I know that you are as curious as I am about the identity of these guys. I sure hope these are the bad guys." He dismounted and holstered his pistol to have a closer look at things. The riders were all heavily armed with plenty of extra ammo. Elmer studied the faces as close as possible in the rain and when he came to the third man he thought the face tripped a memory. Wanted posters were pretty unreliable as a general rule but this mug looked familiar. They searched the men and the horses and came up with dynamite and gold coins and finally, train and stage flyers.

The rain was easing off a little to a steady, quieter downpour. Elmer stood straight and looked at Jack, "I am pretty certain that these are our lads and that they were off to a piece of work. This can't be the whole gang and one got away so we may be having some company along. Hard to tell, they might just cut their losses and wait for a better day.

"We can be pretty sure that there is no one out ahead of us so we can load up these fellows and get back to the stage road. Think that it is time to take the sheriff's advice and get the hell out of these hills. I'd say the sooner, the better."

They set to work to load and truss the dead men over their saddles. Even the mare with the new crease on her head cooperated. The rain continued but daylight remained as they headed back towards the stage road. The rain was slackening as they reached the road and they headed their string east in the direction of Longstreet.

They rode steadily with the weather gradually clearing and the sun coming out. Elmer was leading the string of horses down the middle of the road and Jack kept a close eye on the trail behind and the high ground around, especially to the south of the road. Jack moved up alongside Elmer and cleared his throat, "What are you thinking? Should we find a spot well off the road to pull up for a spell and get some grub into us and catch a few hours of sleep?"

Elmer shrugged and replied, "If I had my druthers I'd ride all night straight back into town and study some wanted posters to identify these fellas but yours is probably a better idea for getting there in one piece. When that moon comes out, and I believe it will tonight, riding down the middle of this road is going to present a nice target to a man with a rifle. And if we do get jumped in that fashion we wouldn't really have much of a chance to even fight back. I reckon these outlaw horses can stand around with a load for a few hours before we finish the ride. Why don't we keep a eye out for a nice cut away to the north and then you can scout around. See if you can find a secluded spot that would be fairly easy to defend."

He paused then, shaking his head. "Still find it hard to believe that we are being pursued but we just can't leave that to chance," he said. "Even with vengeance aside, the rest of the gang is likely to be missing the bag with the schedules and the dynamite. So, scout around and cut away when you find something promising." With that he produced a cigar and a match and fired up.

Jack nodded and roamed ahead, taking care to glance now and then at the back trail for any sign of pursuit. Twenty minutes later he saw what appeared to be a game trail that bore further inspection. He waved to Elmer and pushed off the road into the rocks. It was pretty easy going as he worked his way forward because there was a trail of sorts through the boulders and rocks. Jack was searching for good access to higher ground. Around the base of a crumbling wall he found patches of grass, clumps of bushes and then a spring. There was a slope with more good grass and a reasonably easy assent to higher ground. He climbed for a while, winding around the elevation until he reached a good-sized clearing. It looked like plenty of other fellows before them had found the clearing to be a pretty good camp site.

The higher ground above the campsite looked interesting so he dismounted and climbed around the rocks and brush until he reached the top. There was a good view back the way he had come and he guessed his perch to be about one hundred fee of elevation above the camp site clearing where his horse waited. This looked like a good place to hole up for a few hours and they could defend the camp in the event of trouble. He retraced his steps and rode back to fetch Elmer. He stopped now and again to grab some heavier dry brush for a fire.

By the time they got back to the clearing the sun was almost down. They built a small fire and finished chow with the moon rising. Elmer fired up another cigar and they talked for a bit about the stunning events of the day. The outlaw mounts moved around restlessly with their loads, but it had been a relaxed ride so it was decided that a few more hours would be within their limits. Jack indicated the spot he had climbed to see the back trail but they decided that they were pretty well sheltered from sight right down in the clearing. Elmer volunteered to take the first watch. He moved well away from the fire to sit on a flat rock.

Jack looked around for just the right place for a nap. He found a nice spot within sight of the fire nestled on three sides by boulders. He grabbed the shotgun and the saddlebag with dynamite and cigars along with the saddle and bedroll and curled up with his boots on since it was going to be a short night. He took a last look over Elmer's way and then dozed off to dream about the doctor's daughter Lizzy.

Things weren't going that well for Jack in the dream as Lizzy seemed to have other plans and Jack was moving and talking to her in slow motion. Suddenly Jack was snapped awake by gunfire exploding in the moonlight. A glance at Elmer was enough to tell that he was hit and probably badly as he fell forward with his cigar tumbling away in a little fiery arc.

Jack had a stick of dynamite in his fist as Elmer came to rest and other sounds came through the night air. There were probably a couple of guys, at least, moving forward towards the fire. Jack tossed the stick of explosive at the campfire and it rolled in as he swung the shotgun up for action and pulled back both hammers. There were a couple of stray shots as the gunmen tried to find his position and then the dynamite tore a bright hole in the night. Jack was shielding his eyes from the fire to protect his vision and he managed a pretty good look at the forms of the advancing shooters. He saw at least three of them keeping some space between themselves so he squeezed one trigger. In almost the same second he had shifted his aim and pulled the second trigger. The two shots blended into one shattering roar, and two of the shooters were jerked off their feet and back by the force of the double ought. Terrible screams of pain echoed through the clearing.

The third shooter was holding himself funny but busy trying to find a good target as Jack dropped the shotgun and pulled two revolvers. Jack felt a rock chip from the gunman's next shot as he moved forward low and into the open. He waited patiently and was rewarded when the third shooter left cover for another shot.

Jack emptied both six-shooters at the form of the gunman and saw him pitch to the left in a way that appeared more involuntary then intended. Jack counted him out and pulled up to listen and reload one pistol. He could hear at least one other person moving out there past the edge of the clearing. It sounded as though he was hurrying, maybe away down the slope. It didn't take a lot of figuring for Jack to come up with a plan of action. The only course that made sense was to end this affair here and now. If he could help it there would not be one or more revenge bound gunmen dogging him all the way back to Longstreet and maybe beyond. The surviving robbers would likely backtrack before they regrouped, and Jack knew a great vantage point over that back trail.

He took a last listen and then stepped out to confirm the outlaw casualties. He found them quickly in the moonlight and put a revolver round into each for insurance. He then hurried over to check on Elmer. Jack thought he found a pulse but Elmer was unconscious and hurt bad.

Jack retrieved the still burning cigar and clamped it in his teeth, trying not to choke. He ran back across the clearing to his bedroll where he grabbed his rifle and an extra cigar along with three more sticks of dynamite out of the saddlebag. He took time to light the new cigar off Elmer's, as the fire had been blown apart, and clamped it in his teeth as he took off at a run towards the hill he had climbed a few hours before. He had the help of the moonlight as he hurried upwards through the scree and brush.

Arriving at the top he laid his rifle on a rock and nursed the glowing tip of the cigar. He was in position to cover a large chunk of the trail. He listened intently. He was rewarded almost immediately by the sound of one man yelling and a number of running horses.

He could make out at least two riders with other horses strung between them. He waited for a second before he lit the first fuse. He tossed the stick at what he thought would be about twenty-five feet in front of the first horse and then lit the second fuse. He lobbed the second stick as close as he could at the tail of the last horse. The first stick exploded in a wall of fire and deafening roar.

Jack picked up the rifle and looked down the barrel for a target in the front as the second stick of dynamite went off a good twenty feet behind the trotting string of animals. The first horse was bucking wildly and had wheeled around backwards as the rider struggled for control. Jack waited a moment for a good shot. As the mount settled Jack fired. The rider jerked abruptly to the side and fell to the ground.

As Jack turned his rifle towards the only other rider he saw that the outlaw was unhorsed and starting to run for the shelter of the cliff as he snapped off a shot in Jack's general direction. Jack hunched a little and fired one shot at the runner's legs. The man pulled up and turned for a more careful shot. He must have realized that he couldn't make it to cover and Jack put a round in his heart and then hit him again almost before he hit the ground. Turning a fraction, Jack put the sight on the body of the first rider and squeezed off another round. He figured that there was no sense taking any chances.

The horses had bucked and plunged but were held in place by the amount of scree on either side of the trail. The horses appeared to be all right except for one that had jumped in the rocks and looked to be hurt bad. It was trying to move and making quite a racket. Jack drew a bead on it and shot it and then shot it again for good measure.

He smoked and watched the scene below while he reloaded. He realized that he was exhausted. He offered vague thanks that things had turned out the way they had, except for his partner. He grabbed the rifle and headed back down the hill to see about Elmer.

Jack found Elmer still breathing and unconscious. Jack couldn't see very good in the moonlight, but Elmer appeared to be hit at least twice, in the left shoulder and low on the left side. He was also seeping blood from a head wound, which might have happened when he fell. Jack wiped him up a little with a kerchief and tried to make him comfortable. As Jack straightened up and looked around he worked out a plan. He had to try to get Elmer to a doctor in time and he had to get all these bodies loaded to take along. He took a deep breath and set to work.

After checking that the original three shooters were dead Jack saddled his horse. He rode cautiously back down the approach slope and around the trail back the way they had come the night before. Soon he came upon the havoc he'd created with the dynamite and rifle from above. He found and rounded up four saddle horses and one pack animal. He loaded and tied down the two dead men and led the whole string back to the camp.

Jack unloaded the packhorse, finding rope, axes and a shovel among other things. He loaded the outlaws and gathered all the bedrolls and saddlebags. He saddled Elmer's horse. He thought it might be best for Elmer to sit upright as long as there was no material for a travois. There were no trees close that he could recall and he didn't think that he had any time to waste looking. He stacked and lashed bed rolls and saddlebags on top of Elmer's saddle horn and then loaded Elmer with his face forward on the stacked rolls. Then he tied his partner in place as best he could and braced him with rifles that were lashed to the saddle and to each other. Jack was tired and drenched in sweat but he had made good time and figured he was ready. He had ten horses now tied in a line behind him as he started the return to the coach road.

Dawn was breaking as Jack and his long string wound slowly through the rocks. He took it real slow until they got to the road when he quickly reconfigured the entourage into two strings of five and set off for Longstreet at the best pace that he felt the mounts could manage. He pushed straight through and hit town by mid-afternoon.

There was no problem drawing attention to himself. An inquiry got him to the doctor's office where he banged on the door. It was answered by a middle aged woman who said she would send the doctor out. Jack started untying Elmer from his perch. The doctor arrived, and after glancing at the wounds, he helped Jack pull Elmer off the horse. The physician glanced around at the grisly scene in front of his house and then at Jack who was covered with dried blood and mud and dust but didn't say anything except, "You get the legs, if you will." They carried the unconscious detective into the house and laid him on a table.

Jack watched as the doctor cut away the clothing to examine the wounds. "I know that you are worried about your friend here but I really want you to get out of that shirt and get washed up a bit if you are going to stay here in my operating room. The less dirt around these wounds, the better chance this fella will make it. I'm afraid it's going to be nip and tuck to save him."

Jack nodded as he backed away. "His name's Elmer, Doc, and I hope you can put him back right. He's a good man."

Jack walked out to the kitchen where he found the woman of the house. He stripped his shirt off and washed his face and hands in the sink. The woman was quiet but handed him a clean shirt and he strode back towards the operating room. She followed, and they both watched the doctor work and helped as necessary.

The doctor stopped and spoke to Jack. "Your friend has a head wound that's not too serious, a shattered shoulder where the bullet missed the heart and an abdominal wound that is worrisome and may or may not be bad. There's a clean exit, and it appears like the main organs were spared. The fact that he is still alive and good color would suggest that the damage just might be survivable. The furrow on the hip is ugly but like the head wound it should be fine. If we can just get some liquids into him he might make it, although it will be a long recovery."

Jack's relief surprised him a little. Jack realized that he had become kind of fond of his new friend. His relief at the positive news let him relax a little and he felt how exhausted he was. His growling stomach reminded him that he had eaten nothing since last night. He thanked the doctor and his wife and went back to the kitchen for a drink of water and his shirt. By the time he got to the front door the woman of the house was admitting the sheriff who had the look of a man who was in shock.

"For the love of God, McGill, what the hell have you got parked out in the street?" He nodded to the woman. "Sorry,

Mary. It looks like we are going to need to enlarge the cemetery!
I noticed that you did some work with my old shotgun. And,
what's this? It looks like ole Elmer shot to pieces. You two left
here a week ago loaded with good advice and dynamite and it
appears like you started a war. Is Elmer going to make it?"

The doctor gave a affirmative nod to the last question.
Jack touched the sheriff's elbow and nodded towards the door.
"Come on, Sheriff. Lets leave these good people to their work
and I'll fill you in on what happened when we get outside." Jack
nodded to the doctor and Mary with a grateful smile and followed
the old lawman out the door.

They stood there looking at the herd of horses and the
macabre cargo. There were about thirty other people taking in the
scene close up and considerably more gawking from a distance.
Jack turned to the sheriff and said, "Let's talk as we walk this
bunch to where they can be unloaded. They're past due for water,

feed, and some currying. Elmer and I loaded that short string yesterday afternoon in the rain."

They took Jack's mount and the two strings in tow and the sheriff led the way to the coffin maker's shop.

Jack continued, "We had just found an interesting spot for monitoring the stage road when a storm broke and we had to find cover. We ran into these fellas and got four out of five in a shootout. The ten gauge played a large role. We weren't entirely sure what we had but one had gotten away and we decided to play it conservative and head for town. We laid to in what looked like a pretty good spot for a few hours rest. It's possible that we were in one of the gang's favorite lay bys because they snuck right up on Elmer standing guard and shot the hell out of him, as you just saw yourself. I put the shotgun and the dynamite to work and got lucky."

He fell silent as they stopped at a carpentry shop. As they hitched the horses Jack added, "I'm about tuckered out and I'm hungry enough to eat a horse and chase the rider, present company excepted, of course."

The sheriff was studying him with a wry smile as he answered, "We will have to talk at length later. I'll get things started here and round up some paper work to see if we can identify these characters. You go ahead and head for the hotel for some grub and something to wet your whistle. Might be a good idea to wire the railroad so see if they have anything on that gang that would be helpful. Also think that I will venture that you may well be about the luckiest fellow that I ever ran into. There are some rumors floating around about some other scrapes you've got into. Maybe you should be giving some thought to what you are going to do when that luck thins out on you."

Jack fetched the shotgun and shells from his mount and gave them to the sheriff along with a wide grin by way of response. He turned and led his horse towards the livery on the way to the hotel.

Jack sat alone at the hotel, waiting for dinner and working his way through a bucket of beer that had been sent over from the saloon. The beer was delicious but Jack felt uncomfortable with everyone openly staring at him. He realized again that he really didn't care for that kind of attention. Seemed like a fellow in this line of work might have to be moving on all the time as long as he stayed alive. It must be that or you constantly felt like a target, at least of scrutiny. Jack was almost through the food when the sheriff arrived. The lawman pulled up a chair and helped himself to the beer.

After a good pull on the beer the sheriff spoke. "I'm pretty sure I've got posters on at least five of those dead men. I had an exchange with the railroad and we are damn sure that this is the gang that has been in their hair for so long. They are going to mail me some posters I'm missing. Right now it looks like you got them and a damn good chance that you got all of them. I can't be absolutely sure yet but between the individual rewards and the rewards offered by the stage company and the railroad, I would hazard a guess that you could be picking up about fifteen or twenty thousand dollars here. That's quite a haul for a young fellow for a week's work. When Elmer introduced you the other day I really had no idea. You don't look like a one man army but I guess that's just what you are."

Jack gave him a tired grin and said, "Hell, you know how it goes, Sheriff. I got lucky a couple of times and think maybe these guys were a little overconfident back in that hill country. They did have some flat out bad luck, but like you were saying earlier it's got to run out some time. Oh, and by the way, any reward that's coming on this bit of work will be split down the middle with Elmer. Just hope like hell he's alive to enjoy it."

Jack rose to his feet and touched the brim of his hat. "It's been a pleasure, Sheriff, and I'll see you in the morning. Right now I'm going to get a long bath and a good night's sleep. You have a good night." Jack walked out of the dining room with all eyes following him.

Early the next morning, Jack rose and ate a big breakfast before heading off to check on his partner. Elmer was conscious, but still in pretty hard shape. He listened intently as Jack filled him in on the way things had gone since he'd been shot at the clearing. He whispered his thanks and Jack joked around with him a bit before he left the patient to rest and recover. Jack had a better feeling that Elmer might make it.

The sheriff had just made some fresh coffee when Jack arrived at the jail to check on the paperwork. There was little news except that the money should be at the bank in a few days. They chatted for a while and then Jack left for the hotel. He thought he'd just as well take the money he'd left in the hotel safe the week before and transfer all of it to the bank, at least for as long as he waited for the railroad. He wondered what the dickens he was going to do with all that money. He had a lot on his mind as he walked into the hotel but thought to go to the front desk and get his money belt. Then he headed upstairs to his room.

He reached for the doorknob when the door of the room next to his opened and out stepped Amy, the gun toting farmwoman. She was dressed in her town clothes, all ruffles and bustles, and she made quite a picture. They were both speechless, standing there starring at each other in the hall. Jack reached to pull the brim of his hat while they both glanced around to see if they were being observed. She had her finger to her lips as she motioned Jack to enter her room. She closed the door behind them and turned to face Jack with her hands raised, palms up in front of her as though to warn him to keep his distance.

Jack was the first to speak. "You are a sight for sore eyes. What in the dickens are you doing in this town?"

"Well, in the first place, Mister, I have as much right as anyone to be in this town. But actually, we just arrived here yesterday. My husband, James Brenner, is off to his cousin's ranch about sixty miles to the south of here to buy some horses and borrow a breed bull. He left me here to shop a little and catch up on my reading.

You might as well know that we weren't in this town for two minutes before we were hearing wild stories about you and all your gun slinging. I swear the territory is going to run out of outlaws if you keep this up. Seemed to me like some of the womenfolk were just a little hot and flustered at the very thought of your manly self. I suspect that the preacher will need to say something to them at Sunday service since it's his young wife that seems especially flushed at the thought of you."

Jack had been half listening to her but mostly just drinking her in; savoring her bewitching beauty. He stepped towards her and put his hand on her breast. He said softly, "You talk too much. And I sure don't remember you wearing this many clothes."

She gave him a severe look and pushed his hand away. "If you think for a minute …"

Jack out a hand on each breast and pushed her up against the door. He kissed her on the lips and then the ear and moved to her neck as he pushed harder against her. She was panting as she threw her arms around his neck.

She gasped, "I'm starving to death. I've got to get something to eat or I'll faint!"

Jack muttered into her cleavage, "Don't you worry. If you faint, I'll take care of you. Now let's get you out of this rigging so I can see you better."

An hour later, as they lay exhausted in the sheets, she reached over and took his hand, bringing it to her lips. She gently bit his thumb and said, "If you don't let me out of this room so I can go eat I am going to chew your fingers off. Now, unhand me, you brute" She rolled over on top of him for a long kiss and then scrambled out of the bed to her feet. "I doubt they have enough food to satisfy me. Maybe I'll come back here and have you for dessert." She giggled and then put her hands up to hide her nakedness from his hungry eyes.

Jack rose also and gave her a final naked hug before he turned to his own clothes. Picking up the money belt he thought about it and then tossed it over by her rifle in the corner. He glanced out the window and down into the alley behind the hotel as he buttoned his shirt.

"It's a nice sunny afternoon and I'm hungry now myself. You do wear a man out with your goings on. I'm going to leave that money belt here. If I don't make it back you can buy yourself a nice dress. I'll have the people downstairs send some grub over to the tavern where I'll wash it all down with a couple of beers. I don't know how much shopping you have planned but maybe we could meet back up here in a couple of hours and talk about your favorite book or something." He pulled on his boots as she came up behind him and put her arms around him.

"I don't think you care a hoot about my reading, but you'll say anything to get me in that bed again. Just because I'm a girl alone doesn't mean you can take advantage. You might notice I've got my rifle with me." She hugged herself against him then and said softly, "I might sound silly here but you are only the second man I've ever been with. You have ruined me. I had no idea I could be this happy." Her stomach rumbled and she staggered over to the door. "I'll look in the hall. I can't wait to see you again." She blew him a kiss and opened the door, looking both ways before motioning him out. Jack took the opportunity to fondle her breast in passing as she glared at him. She smacked his bottom and watched him stride down the hall towards the stairs.

Amy waited for a minute before closing the door and heading for the dining room. She hoped they served a robust lunch. Jack was gone by the time she reached the first floor. She wondered what in the devil she was going to do but decided that she could think better with some food in her.

Jack took his mug of beer to a table at the rear of the tavern by the back door. He liked to have a view of the whole room and figured that was one of the changes in this new life of his. It didn't seem like he had much time to think about things anymore because things were happening too fast and he just went with it like a tumbling weed. In his old life there had been more than enough time to mull things over and now he kind of missed that. He guessed that change couldn't be helped.

He had a second beer before the sandwiches arrived. He took his time, finally raising his mug to signal the barkeep to bring one more. He nursed this beer, looking into the foam and thinking about this woman. Now that he had been with her again he wondered if he could walk away from her. He tried to talk sense to himself but not with much success. He couldn't have her but she stirred him in a way that he had never been stirred before.

Jack felt someone coming and looked up to see the sheriff approaching with a big grin. "Are you crying in your beer," he said, "thinking about how hard it's going to be to spend all that money? What a life! Well, more tough news for you, Jack, cause I was digging through all that gear on those horses and found a wanted poster that fit one of the dead men. Maybe he was proud of it. But, whatever, the asshole was wanted for rape and murder and bank robbery and the reward on him is two thousand, dead or alive! I would let you buy me a couple of beers but that will have to wait till later, Gotta git across town to see the old widow woman who claims the lads are stealing her onion sets out of her garden. I just wanted to give you the good news."

"Thanks, sheriff. Whenever you're thirsty you look me up. Give my best to the widow woman." Jack watched the sheriff leave and then resumed musing about Amy. He knew that she was making him a little crazy. He wondered idly if he could get away with calling her husband out in a gunfight but that didn't have a very good taste to it, especially if he then ran off with the new widow.

He knew that he wasn't thinking very clearly and then he felt the presence of someone right in front of him at the same time that he heard the back door open behind him. He looked up to see Stretch standing right in front of him with a rifle in his right hand pointed straight at Jack's heart. Stretch was wearing a smile as big as all outdoors, and Jack felt a guy on either side behind his chair. He felt a gun barrel at the base of his neck and then his revolvers were being removed from the holsters. His hands were jerked behind him and quickly secured with a rawhide strip.

Stretch leaned across the table and drove the barrel of the rifle into Jack's belly. Jack doubled forward a little and gasped. Stretch rasped, "You yell or make a fuss and I'll beat you to death right here with this rifle butt. Grady put me on the payroll and sent me out to try to pick up your trail. You shouldn't be surprised to hear that you weren't very hard to find. Such a hero you turned out to be. Guess you were thinking that nobody could take you. Ain't you something? I want to kill you so bad I can taste it, but Grady is going to be mighty generous when I throw your carcass at his feet. Now, get up real slow and we're all going to go for a little trip. Parks, check out the back and we'll all leave together out in the alley."

Jack was busy studying his chances and decided that he would have to wait for something better than these odds. He stumbled out the door with the three in close company.

Stretch was talking, "This is your lucky day, McGill. See how I thought to bring along an extra mount so we didn't have to bother with your horse." He covered Jack with the rifle and said to the others, "Dig through his pockets for any money and then get him up and get him lashed tight to the stirrups." He took the money, about seventy-five dollars, and stood back to keep an eye out. "Pull that slicker out of the saddlebag and tie it around his shoulders so nobody can see he's hogtied. I'll have the reins, asshole, so just give me any excuse. Keep your head down!"

Saying that, he drove the butt of the rifle into Jack's belly and Jack jerked forward, the air pushed out of him.

Stretch handed Parks a gold piece and said, "Get a couple of days grub and a couple of bottles of whiskey and meet us a few miles out of town on the coach road back to Wakefield. Hurry up and keep your head down. Especially stay clear of that sheriff. These folks would be all upset if anything happened to their hero here."

Parks mounted and took off. Stretch rode over to Jack and took his mount's reins and then drove an old hankerchief into Jack's mouth to keep him silent and led the way down the alley in the opposite direction. Jack heard a window opening and looked up to see the back of the hotel.

Amy was standing at the window of her room looking right at him. Her expressive eyes were flashing with anger. Jack shook his head no but she had stepped away and then was back, and just as he had feared she had the rifle. She banged it on the sill and in a loud voice said, "Stop right there or you're dead. Cut that man loose or I'll shoot. Do you hear me?"

Stretch pulled up at the voice and turned to the window saying, "What the hell! Put that gun down, you crazy bitch!" Jack knew the guy bringing up the rear had his gun out and was moving around to find a shot. Jack tried to knee his mount to ruin the aim. Amy was busy looking at Stretch and never saw the gun until it was too late. The pistol went off next to Jack's ear and he saw Amy was hit high in the chest, driven back into the room. Jack felt a bolt of pain such as he had never experienced. He felt like his heart had broken, and he was convulsed with sobs.

Stretch was looking at Jack and guessing the truth and he started to belt him again but didn't. Instead he cursed his partner. "You dumb son of a bitch. You killed that bitch and now we'll swing from a rope if we don't get the hell out of this town. Let's go!" They lashed their horses down the alley. They reached the road and rode hard for a few miles before Stretch led the way off the track and up a nearby hill. They pulled up where they could still see the road and waited. Jack finally was able to spit out the rag. Stretch noticed but didn't replace it.

Stretch was still pissed and turned on his partner. "You're dumber than a wagon tongue, Cheney. Now Parks will never get out of that town. Sure as hell we was all seen together and now that bitch is murdered. She wouldn't have done nothing anyway. She'd a been afraid of shooting her boyfriend here." Stretch nodded at Jack and then just shook his head in disgust as he watched the stage road. After a while Stretch dismounted and had Cheney provide cover while Stretch untied Jacks hands and retied them in front and secured them to the saddle horn. He was checking the leg ties when he found the hidden gun. He dug it out and put it in his pocket but said nothing. He backed up and studied Jack for a moment and then turned away to remount.

A half hour passed very slowly before Parks galloped into sight. Cheney rode out to flag him down, and they gathered on the backside of the knoll as Stretch took the lead in a northerly direction out into the hills. He yelled back to Parks, "What the hell happened back in that town, anyway?"

Parks moved closer before he said, "It was all kind of confusing. Some gal got shot or shot herself at the hotel and she was in bad shape. Hell, maybe she's dead by now. The talk was that she was in real rough shape but still breathing. Everybody was running around yelling. Lots of excitement! They couldn't find their hero, here, and nobody seemed to know where he'd gone to. I mean, they seen us leaving the bar by the back door but they must not have seen our faces very good because nobody asked me about it and I just went on about my business. I did hear talk that the gal what got shot was a real good-looking bitch." Stretch said nothing and after a quick glance at Jack he turned forward and kept them to a steady pace.

Part IV

Southfork

Riding along silently Jack considered what his options might be and really couldn't see that he had any options. The lashings were good and tight and he was being led to the slaughter unless some unknown got thrown into the mix. He couldn't figure what Stretch was up to, him knowing about the thirty-two and not saying or doing anything. Stretch didn't strike Jack as a deep thinker of any kind so why did the freight hauler seem to be trying so hard to figure something out?

Jack gave up that line of thought and turned his mind back to Amy. He knew in his heart she was dead, and he was determined to put a bullet in Cheney before the end. He almost barked a bitter laugh at his last thought. As unlikely as that seemed, Jack knew that he would never give up, at least not until it was over when he was dead or free. In the meantime might as well enjoy the scenery, just in case this turned out to be his last ride.

Stretch called a halt at dusk and they made camp. They untied Jack from the stirrups and pulled him off to walk to the nearest tree. Stretch fashioned a noose on the end of a lariat and slipped it over Jack's head where he tightened it a little. Then he threw the other end of the rope over a branch about ten feet high and took the free end that descended around the tree and threw it up over another branch on the backside of the tree. He ordered Jack to sit and then took up most of the slack before securing the rope to a third branch. Then he tied Jack's feet together and told his Parks and Cheney to fix some grub. He winked at Jack, picked up his rifle and walked over to the campfire.

The abductors passed the bottle around and eventually got around to eating. In due course Parks brought Jack some grub and a canteen but although they joked among themselves on the subject, they wasted no whiskey on the prisoner. Jack wondered what was going on with Stretch and he fell asleep without coming to any good answer,

They broke camp a little after dawn and headed north, wending their way through the hills in the direction of Southfork. They stayed well clear of any settlements and mostly stayed off the any roads they came to. Stretch followed his instructions, taking care to avoid witnesses to this exercise. Grady had emphasized that there be no trail back to the ranch in the event that Stretch had some success. The foreman had given Stretch a string of horses and fifty bucks so he could stay out for a month and see what he could find of the cowboy.

Stretch had a notion that his capture of McGill was going to be quite a shock to the ranch foreman and old man Wilson. That was before they had any notion of how famous the young cowboy had become in the last month. Stretch couldn't help but wonder where all the reward money had gone to. McGill had less than a hundred dollars on him when they grabbed him. He figured that they might never know and he figured for certain that they would never get any information out of McGill. The fella never said a word, just studying his captors like a caged animal.

Stretch recalled that time he had dogged McGill's trail out of Southfork after their confrontation in the street. He'd always wondered why McGill hadn't killed him back then in the woods. It would have been so smart to take care of things, and no witnesses. Instead McGill let an enemy live who would eventually hunt him down. Made no sense, as this cowboy sure had no problem with killing people. Well, thought Stretch, not just people, but thieves and killers. It was all very hard to figure and mostly he tried to push all of that stuff out of his mind.

On the afternoon of the third day they were riding through the hills south of Southfork. They pushed west a few miles to avoid any contact before Stretch headed them north again in the direction of the Wilson ranch. The Wilson home place seemed awfully quiet as they rode into the yard and up to the large main house.

Stretch dismounted and went to the door. An old grizzled fellow in a dirty cook's apron answered the door and led Stretch into the house.

Parks turned to Cheney. "What do ya bet that we're in for a big bonus for this catch?" He jerked his head towards Jack. Cheney shrugged, but his confident smile revealed his thinking.

Stretch reappeared with an impressive looking man. His dress and carriage bespoke power and money, and plenty of both. Hank Wilson stepped to the edge of the porch and studied Jack with what, on the surface, appeared to be a complete lack of emotion. He spoke in a hard rasp, "Welcome to the end of the line, cowhand. Actually, you will be better off to think of it as hell. Quite frankly, you murdering scum, I am going to hurt you almost as much as you wounded me." He turned to Stretch, "Good work, Connor. Tie him up on the open wall in the carriage barn. Give him food and water to keep up his strength for his last days. I'll stop down later to check on things. I'll have the cook bring you down a bottle and some makings."

Wilson returned to the house and Stretch led the group across the yard to the large wagon barn. They pulled Jack off the horse and marched him into the barn. Stretch replaced the noose around Jack's neck and threw the other end of the rope over a rafter and dogged it down so he could just sit down. They tied his feet securely from the back and kept his hands tied in front so he could do his business without being untied. They gave him a drink of water and then left him alone. Then the guards made themselves comfortable with smokes and whiskey while they waited for the chow bell. The mood was quite festive as Parks and Cheney speculated about the size of the reward. Their hopes were soaring with the whiskey.

After dinner Wilson arrived at the barn with a quirt in his hand and stopped to study Jack for a while before approaching him. Jack could smell the whiskey on his breath and braced himself. Tapping his left palm with the quirt Wilson spoke softly. "When I was young I spent time at sea, and I once saw a fellow flogged to death for striking an officer. That was quite a death and worth consideration.

"However, years later, I witnessed a thief skinned alive by some buffalo hunters and, I'm afraid that I liked the knife work better than the cat-o-nine. It is your misfortune, cowboy, that I really like to hurt my enemies. But, I don't want to go on and on. I just wanted you to know that much." He stopped speaking. With his eyes locked on Jack's he produced a wicked looking knife from under his coat and turned it. The knife had a strange curved blade and finished in a needlepoint. Jack had never seen one like it.

Wilson locked Jack's right wrist in an iron grip and pushed the point of the dagger through the shirtsleeve on the upper arm. The knife had to be sharp as a razor because as he pulled it down it seemed to fall through the material rather than cut it. Wilson withdrew the knife and reached out to rip a swath of material from the shirt arm. He grabbed Jack's arm again and deftly pushed the tip of the blade under the skin and out again an inch away. There was very little blood until he started pulling the blade down the outside of the bicep. Jack gasped as the blade was pulled free again. The rancher wiped the blood on Jack's shirt and put the knife away.

He looked into Jack's eyes with what passed for a smile and said, "I've had some practice but need more. I am so looking forward to this. But not yet." He was turning to leave and then stopped. "I promised Grady that I would wait for him," he said. "He was very close to my son and he shares my fascination with pain, although he is more thuggish, if you will. But when he has softened you a little, you and I will get back to that arm. Have a great night, cowboy. Grady should be back tomorrow afternoon." Wilson turned again and walked out of the barn.

Jack craned forward to study his arm wound as the guards moved forward to do the same. Cheney laughed and whistled in appreciation. "This is going to be sweet, you asshole!" He glanced behind him and then turned and drove his fist into Jack's belly. As Jack doubled over against the noose Stretch jerked Cheney around landed a roundhouse on the side of his jaw, driving him to the floor in a heap. Jack was gagging as Cheney rolled away holding the side of his head and trying to right himself. Cheney reached back for his revolver but Stretch already had his rifle up and ready.

Cheney screamed in rage, "What the hell you want to go and do that, you son of a bitch? What are you doing, protecting him?"

"That's exactly what I'm doing, you stupid bastard! I'm getting reward money from Grady and Wilson for bringing this asshole back in one piece and good shape. I'll tell you what though, you give me a couple hundred dollars and you can do anything you want with the cowboy. Since I know that you don't have a penny in your pocket you can keep your damn distance."

Cheney saw the logic in that, or most of it, and with an unforgiving glare in Stretch's direction, he backed away and out of the barn. Jack had fallen into a sitting position and he just stayed there. It was going to be a long night and he couldn't figure what Stretch was up to, but he knew that whatever it was that it wouldn't make much difference. Time was definitely running out and his upper arm was oozing blood.

Grady rode late in the afternoon the following day. He tied up at the wagon barn and stood there for a moment, enjoying the scene before him of the trussed up cowboy in the noose. He clapped his old drinking buddy on the shoulder and exclaimed, "Stretch, you old son of a whore, you're good for something besides steering a wagon, ain't ya? Look what we got here. We got us a puncher that looks a little the worse for wear."

Grady advanced on Jack who looked straight ahead and tried to put himself in another place and time. Grady interfered with that by slapping Jack back and forth across the face with his leather gloves. He leaned in close to the prisoner and spat out, "I guarantee you that you are going to live through this night no matter how much you scream for death." Grady then pushed his knee into Jack's groin just hard enough to hurt and drove his fist up into the bottom of Jack's ribs on the right side. Jack thought he felt a rib crack as the sick feeling from the groin hit spread through him.

Grady chuckled and slapped him a few more times with the gloves. Then he stepped back and studied Jack with a wide smile and shiver of anticipation.

"Yeah, Stretch, you did real good here! I'd say we got us an evening's entertainment ahead of us. No, that would be wrong. We are going to wind this out for a couple of days, easy. Get some water and lanterns together while I run up to the house and talk to the boss. I'll fetch some whiskey for you lads and get you some money for your work." So saying, Grady strode off for the ranch house, whistling a merry tune.

Stretch barked orders at his men, sending them in different directions for buckets of water and lanterns. Stretch then turned and advanced on the prisoner who was studying him closely. The hauler pulled out his sheath knife and bent to slash the rawhide around Jack's boots. He drove the knife in the dirt and then reached around behind him to produce the thirty-two caliber. Stretch then jerked up Jack's right pant leg and replaced the revolver in the clip. Not a word had been said as Stretch leaned his rifle against the wall and loosened the noose so while it was still in place Jack could easily toss it off his head. Stretch then retrieved the knife and proceeded to saw through the underside of the hide strip that bound Jack's hands. Jack's wrists were raw from the hide but Stretch held his hands together and smoothed the hide strip so it would appeared the Jack was still tied.

After a glance around, Stretch spoke softly, "Think it's best that you sit on your haunches when the time comes and we'll see what happens. I been thinking about this for a week now, it seems, and I've made my choice. Can't run from this thing or the hunting will commence again. Someone has to die here tonight so here's my deal. You kill Grady and I'll back your play the best I can. I ain't no gunslinger like you and I'd never have the sand to brace Grady. I've seen what he's done to other fellas and I'd freeze up tighter than a bug's ass. Think I'll find my courage when Grady's done for. Maybe we'll live through this night, Cowboy."

Stretch grabbed his rifle, winked at Jack and walked over to his favorite crate where he sat and started rolling a smoke. Jack was wondering at the lack of information in that speech he'd just listened to but was getting nowhere. He had been feeling pretty resigned to his fate, and now, thanks to the hauler, he might have a chance. He might never find out why Stretch had changed sides this late in the game. Grady really did have a mental edge on this freight hauler and it was still at least four guns to two.

Cheney and Parks returned with buckets of water and lanterns. They lit the lanterns and hung them on posts and then they made themselves comfortable and rolled smokes. They were happily speculating on the size of the payout and anxious for the arrival of the whiskey promised by Grady.

Another hour passed before Grady strode back into the wagon barn with a couple of bottles. He handed them around with a pouch of coins for each man. Then he turned to Jack and smacked his hands together. Grady grabbed the bottle from Cheney and took a long pull before returning it and moving in Jack's direction. He laughed and said, "I'm coming, Cowboy, so say your prayers. Just as quick as the boss gits here we're gonna have us a party."

Jack had settled in a squat. Now he flicked the noose off and pulled up the pant leg at the same time, seizing the concealed pistol. The giant foreman moved quick for a big man and he was moving now with a roar while he clawed at his side for his own sidearm. Jack was calculating that a gut shot man was a dead man even if the slug didn't stop him cold. Out of the corner of his eye Jack saw Cheney drop the bottle as he went for his six-gun.

Jack put four rounds into Grady's lower belly and the big man fetched up right in front of the squatting cowboy. Jack heard a rifle shot and watched Grady grab his lower gut with a bellow of anguish and rage. He knew he was a dead man and reached for his killer. Jack pointed the revolver straight up at Grady's throat and fired. The slug traveled through the throat and the head and out the top with a spray of blood and brains.

Jack rolled free of the tumbling giant and saw that Cheney was down and dying and that Parks had grabbed a rifle and was trying to draw a bead on Stretch. Jack and Stretch fired at the same time and Parks flew backwards, dead before he hit the ground.

Jack glanced once more at Cheney before stuffing the revolver in his belt and grabbing Parks' rifle. He stopped to look at Stretch who was grinning with relief.

Jack said, "Got to get Wilson right now to finish this thing."

Stretch jacked in a fresh round and nodded his whole-hearted assent. "I'm right behind you, boss." He laughed and fell in step with his new ally as they hurried out of the barn.

Wilson was running out the front door of the big house waving a revolver in one hand and the skinning knife in the other. He was yelling something that they couldn't understand.

Jack raised the rifle as he leaned against the barn. He squeezed off a round and Wilson staggered, but came on. The rifle spoke again and that brought the old rancher up short. The third shot dropped him right there in the dirt.

Jack said to Stretch, "Go check the bunkhouse and around about to see if we've got any more problems to deal with. There was an old cook around earlier that might need settling. I'll check Wilson and then have a look at the house. It might almost be time for a neighborly drink."

Stretch managed a smile and took off for the bunkhouse at a lope. Jack walked slowly towards Wilson, glancing up at the house from time to time. It was getting darker as the sun set, but Jack could see that the old rancher had fallen on his skinning knife. He was quite dead, and maybe this whole affair was at an end. Jack moved on to the house. He could see nothing moving in the windows but he advanced cautiously, the rifle ready.

Once in the house Jack moved carefully from room to room, listening attentively for any sound. He noted that a wall safe was open in a room lined with bookshelves and dominated by a large desk. Jack figured this must be the office and continued to search each room in the house until he was certain he was alone. Satisfied, he returned to the office for a good look around before he returned to the porch to await Stretch.

His new friend soon returned carrying a lantern and announced that his search had also drawn a blank. Jack produced a bottle and two glasses and indicated that Stretch should have a seat on the stoop.

Jack poured and sipped and cleared his throat carefully. Finally he spoke, "Here we are, and I mean, right here at the crossroads. You and I have to come to some decisions and we don't have much time.

"I don't know why you sided with me and guess that you can say or not, no matter. What's done is done and what we done is shoot the most powerful rancher around and his foreman and a couple of others. There's a lot of money in this house and guess you could say that we aren't exactly leading citizens around here. There is probably a new sheriff in town. Tollliver at the bank would probably speak for me, but I don't really know. My old Uncle Bill, back in Missouri, used to have a saying about not wanting to take some mess or other to the jury. I've got a bad feeling about this whole thing. What do you think?"

Stretch scratched his head and sipped on the whiskey. He replied slowly, "How much money?" His mug split in a big grin. Then, "Hell, McGill, I sided with you cause I remembered when I was a kid I would'a looked up to a fella like you. I like to drink beer and tell tall tales and laugh at a mean asshole like Grady but what they had planned for you was bullshit. Then there was that time I was on your sign and you had me dead to rights but didn't gun me like I would'a gunned you. Still not sure how I did what I did, though, but like you said, it's done. And this is the best whiskey I've ever tasted. That said, I spent the last few years driving big wagons of shit from town to town. I been shot at by Indians and outlaws a few times, but I never killed a man before. I can kind of see what you're saying here, but I ain't no deep thinking gunslinger like you. You figure out a god-damned plan, and that will be our plan."

Jack thought about that little speech for a minute and then made up his mind. "Yeah then, all right Stretch, I reckon I got your drift. Here's what I'm thinking: we got to make it look like we had nothing to do with the killing, like that it was all between them dead guys." He could see that he had all of his partner's attention.

"We are going to take all the money and whatever else we need out of the house and then we are going to burn all the evidence of what happened. Then there will only be our story and nothing to contradict it. Not likely that anyone is going to ride in on us this time of night but we have to adjust our plan if anyone does. So, let's get to it! First we get the loot and whatever supplies we want." Jack drained his glass and got up with Stretch right behind him.

They went first to the ranch office where Stretch whistled at the hoard of gold and paper money. His voice sounded choked. "We are rich! I ain't never seen this much money!" His eyes were the size of saucers as he cupped a hand full of gold. "Jesus Christ, this is so beautiful!"

Jack chuckled and clapped Stretch on the shoulder. "I'm going to give this room and Wilson's room a going over to see if I can turn up anything of interest. You round up two mounts and a packhorse with some good saddlebags. We'd best move right along and keep an ear peeled for company. Meet me back here." Jack headed for the stairs and the bedrooms.

By the time Stretch returned Jack had found an assortment of ghoulish trophies and another few hundred dollars. They loaded the money in a couple of saddlebags and went in search of supplies. They were not disappointed. There was plenty of good grub in storage. When they had the packhorse securely loaded they turned to the task of moving the bodies.

Jack had decided that Wilson's room in the middle of the second floor was the best place for the charade. They patted down the corpses for money and then wrapped them in blankets to move them. It seemed like a good idea not to be covered in blood and to carry the bodies rather than drag them. Grady turned out to be quite a challenge. It was necessary to rig a travois to move the foreman's bulk and Jack walked the horse right into the house, to the foot of the stairs. Stretch rigged a double-block pulley from a beam above the top of the staircase to haul Grady's corpse to the second floor landing. The two partners then dragged chairs into the main bedroom and tied the bodies in sitting positions so what survived would be found thus.

They doused the four corpses with all the coal oil they'd found and all but a few bottles of liquor. They added a couple of buckets of axle grease and all of the extra bacon and grease pots. Jack wanted the bodies as completely burned as possible, figuring that the less that remained the better. They found a stack of posts that they employed to shore up the ceiling of the first floor under the main bedroom to keep the fire upstairs raging as long as possible before everything crashed down.

Finally the two partners decided that they had done about as much as they could do with the funeral pyre. They kept the best of the weapons and plenty of ammunition and threw all the rest into Wilson's bedroom. Then they sat outside on the stoop and poured a drink.

They sipped quietly for a minute before Jack spoke. "I guess that we're ready, or close enough," he said. "To my way of thinking I've got to go into town to cover our tracks and put us in the clear. There's some chance that word of you bringing me here got out, in which case I can't just disappear. I don't want to feel like I'm on the run.

"I'm going to tell the sheriff the truth to a point. I'm going to describe the scene as Grady came into the wagon barn and then say other riders came into yard. At that point Grady left me and looked outside. He told you to watch me and took Parks and Cheney with him to the big house and that's the last we seen of them. After a bit we heard a lot of shooting and you went and looked out but you didn't see nothing so you ran and blew out the lantern and waited. When you heard horses leaving you went out and looked again and horses were gone and the house was all afire. You thought about things for a while but were pretty crazy with the whole turn of events and no money for your work even. You must have been afraid of getting blamed somehow so you saddled a horse and untied me at gunpoint and rode away, most likely to the west and away from the ranch crew. I found a horse and some of my gear and rode into town. Luckily I had a twenty dollar gold piece hidden in my boot."

Jack stopped to polish off his whiskey and rubbed his hands together in satisfaction. "What do you think? The new sheriff might not like that story one bit but what's he going to do with it? He rides out here and there is nothing left but smoldering cinders to consider. You're gone forever and I didn't see anything at all, just heard some stuff. The marks on my wrists will convince anyone that I've been a prisoner for a long time and my arm and rib and other marks will help with my story. My future plans will be to travel back to Longstreet and find out what happened to my girlfriend and Elmer.

"So, that brings us to you and me, Stretch. You and I have a sort of mixed history and actually only been partners for a few hours. Here's what I want you to do. Ride mostly south, kind of following in our tracks up here. About ten to twelve miles south southeast of here is pretty good sized hill with a lot of big old cottonwoods along the side of it. You know the knoll I'm talking about." Here Stretch nodded and Jack continued, "That's where you'll be camped and waiting for me. I should be there no later than tomorrow morning.

"Keep an eye peeled and if it looks like there's some big trouble coming your way then get the hell out of there and head for Longstreet. You can check in at the hotel as John Magrewe so we'll have to grab some better duds for you from Wilson's closet. You can say you're waiting for your brother and headed for California or something. Less said the better and if I'm not there in a week take the money and run. I'd use a new name and start a new life, but that's just me."

Jack paused for a minute and flashed a big grin, saying, "If I catch up with you we'll split the money and have a beer."

Stretch had rolled a smoke and lit up. He was studying Jack and finally spoke up. "I've been around a bit, McGill, and

I'm going to tell you that I've never met anybody quite like you. I ain't proud of switching sides but feel like I changed from the wrong side to the right side. That sounds better. But I sure never dreamed that doing the right thing was going to make me rich.

"I've been on the move since I was about seven years. I know how to drive and drink and whore and not a hell of a lot more than that, really, just mostly getting by stuff. I've never stayed in a hotel or worn nice clothes. If I have to hightail it to Longstreet I'll be waiting there for you. I believe that you are going to have to school me little before I start my new life or I ain't going to last very long."

Jack stood and said, "We're good then. Let's find you a few clothes first and get this place fired up. Think that it's time to get the hell out of here while our luck holds."

Wilson had quite a wardrobe but Stretch settled for well worn pants and coat, a couple of shirts and an old hat and boots.

The fit was close enough to work. They set the fire in the bedroom and walked outside to watch for a while.

Within ten minutes the fire was well along so they turned the horses towards the road to town. After about a mile Stretch found a nice hardscrabble patch and headed his mount and packhorse towards the south. They had decided that it might be bad luck to shake hands (yet another bit of wisdom from Jack's uncle) so they nodded their farewells and parted.

Jack took his time riding to town, even dozing a little as the horse walked towards the faintest signs of dawn. He got to town as the sun rose and looked for a sign for a doctor. Unable to locate a doctor's office, he headed for the house on the north side where he had seen the murdered doctor's lovely daughter on his way out of town.

As he rode slowly his thoughts were a jumble. He didn't know this girl; she had never even spoken to him. He had thought a lot about her in the last month but that didn't mean that she had ever thought of him again. Her father would be long buried and she might well be long gone, probably was. But, what the hell, he thought. Might as well follow it through and then he could put it out of his mind or…that was where he thought about Amy flying back from the window, driven by the force of the slug from Cheney's gun. If he did get through, he wondered what he was going to find when he finally got back to Longstreet. Elmer might have made it but there was little hope that Amy had done so.

Jack arrived at the house he remembered and slowly dismounted, throwing the reins over the picket fence. He knew it was pretty early in the morning but wanted to get this over with, however it went. He knocked lightly on the front door of the little house and waited with hat in hand. Shortly the door opened and the older woman he had seen that last day here was standing there, looking at him curiously.

She spoke first. "I believe that I recognize you from the day of the bank robbery," she said. "You're the gunman who shot the robbers, right? How may I help you?" Her voice and demeanor were guarded, but that seemed only reasonable to Jack.

He replied, "Ma'am, my arm has been cut rather badly and is in need of a dressing of sorts so it doesn't go bad on me. I wouldn't bother you but thought, having seen the old doctor's daughter here, that someone in this house might be able to point me in the direction of some help with a wound. I just now rode into town and could just use a little help."

The woman was measuring him with a critical eye but seemed to come to a judgment and said, "Maybe it wasn't necessary for me to call you a gunman. That does sound rather negative. You did save the bank's money and some of that, a very little bit, was mine, so I should be a little more generous. I should tell you that there is no one left in town of a medical sort now except possibly myself. I have been around it a little and used to assist Lizzy's father when he needed a bit of help. Come on in and let's have a look at that arm." She led the way to the kitchen and the sink where she looked at the wound.

"What an odd cut you've got here! This may hurt a little." She cleaned and trimmed, dismissing the idea of stitches. Finally she dressed and wrapped the wound. "Change the dressing a couple of times," she said, "and then leave it open to the air and just try to keep it clean as best you can. It will leave quite a scar but it looks like it will mend."

Jack was admiring her deft touch. "I sure am grateful to you, Ma'am. What do I owe you for your work?"

She made a dismissive motion as she shook her head. "Let's just call it even for saving the robbery loot." A slight creak of the floorboards made her pause. "Oh, Lizzy, I didn't hear you get up." She stepped around Jack to the doorway and held her arms out to the young woman. They embraced for a few seconds and then turned to Jack.

"You remember, Lizzy, this is the fellow who shot the bank robbers. He came here to get a bad cut fixed up." Her arm was still around the girl who was smiling timidly at Jack. He knew as he gawked at her that this was indeed an uncommon beauty. No words came to mind to do her justice.

The girl said, "I can't thank you for shooting those robbers but I will admit that I am grateful to you for avenging the murder of my father. He was certainly the dearest, gentlest, kindest man I shall ever know, and they shot him down out of spite. I think perhaps that the pain will never go away. I'm so glad that Martha was able to help you and if there is anything else, please ask." She glanced with affection at the older woman who returned the glance and pulled her closer.

Jack watched and tried to take all this in. He wondered just what it was that he was seeing with his own eyes. This was so foreign to him; completely outside any of his experience. These two women were completely at ease with one another and apparently in some sort of love with each other. Was that possible? Apparently it was, because the evidence was right in front of his eyes. As the two women turned to face him again Jack touched the brim of his hat with a little nod. He made a great effort to keep his face neutral and said, "I can't thank you enough for all your help. I sure do wish you the best of luck!" He made his way back towards the front door. He waved and smiled as he rode away in search of the sheriff.

Jack's mind was racing as he rode. He was having a hard time working out what he had just seen but guessed that it didn't much matter. One thing for sure was that Miss Lizzy had no thoughts of him like he might have thoughts about her. He didn't understand but mused that whatever the deal was back there, she was not the girl for him. Now ain't life just a son of a gun?

Jack found his way back to main street and he dismounted in front of the sheriff's office. He could have gone for a big cup of coffee and a stack of flapjacks, but he cleared his throat and banged on the door. He was answered with a yell to come in and he opened the door and smelled the coffee. The man at the desk had a star pinned on and sort of looked like a lawman with the moustache and the extra girth around the middle.

Jack started in, "Morning! You must be the new sheriff."

"I don't recognize you, young fellow, so I'm curious as to how you would know that I'm new here."

"Well sir, I'm not from these parts. I was in this town for a bit about a month ago, and I was just returned to this area against my will. I've got a curious story to tell you if you've got a minute and maybe a cup of that coffee. There's been an incident you will want to know about."

"There's a cup on the sideboard there. Get some coffee and have a seat. The name's Thatcher, Enid Thatcher."

Jack filled a cup and took a seat, saying, "I rode into this town a month ago right in the middle of a bank robbery. I heard shots from down by the livery and saw the sheriff miss with the scattergun and get himself gunned down. I had a nice angle so I plugged the two shooters. I see by your expression the question so I'll tell ya flat. I don't know why I did it, it just seemed like the right thing to do at the time. The banker, Tolliver, told me there'd be hell to pay cause one of the dead guys was the only son of the richest cattleman around here. He gave me a little reward and advised me to hightail it. There was no reason to stay so I lit a shuck, but not before a big fella named Grady, the rancher's foreman, looked me up and promised revenge for the killing. A fella they called Stretch followed me out of town, but I caught onto him and sent him back to town minus his pants and horse, which I sent along later.

"About a week ago that fella Stretch and a couple of others got the drop on me in a town called Longstreet and hauled me back to the ranch trussed up like a turkey. They were very careful not to be seen along the way." Here Jack exhibited his raw wrists to his listener who nodded and gestured to him to continue.

"Well, they tied me up in the wagon barn and fetched old man Wilson. He seemed like a pretty hard fellow and right pleased to have me in hand. He pushed a strange looking knife in my arm here and said he was looking forward to skinning me alive just as quick as Grady took a break from roundup and softened me up real nice. Grady showed up and was just getting into softening me up when we all heard a bunch of horses come into the yard. Grady took a breather from pounding on me and went to look. He barked at Parks and Cheney to follow and left. Shortly we heard a lot of shooting and Stretch went to look and came back and blew out the lanterns. We heard horses leaving and Stretch looked again and said the house was afire. He was all shook up and scared so he cut me loose at gunpoint and rode off towards the southwest. Away from the guys who'd just left and the ranch crew. He was going like a bat out of hell. I watched the fire for a while and then came into town and got this arm looked at by that nice lady named Martha. I thought that you would want to know before I headed back to Longstreet. I got to check on my partner, a stage company detective, who was recovering from some bullet holes he'd acquired during our work together." Jack sipped his coffee.

Thatcher studied Jack for some time before saying, "That's quite a story. It's not really my jurisdiction but guess we could ride out to the ranch and see what we've got. First, let's you and me go over and say hello to Tolliver at the bank. I suspect that Wilson was his best customer." The sheriff stood and waved Jack towards the door.

Tolliver was surprised to see Jack but not unhappy. He grinned at the sheriff, "This lad is quite a citizen, Thatcher. Yes siree, quite the citizen. Just as cool as a cucumber in cream sauce. I will say that I'm surprised to see you again. McGill." When Tolliver heard the news he was astonished. "Who the devil would do such a thing? Who would dare attack the Wilson ranch? Are you thinking about a posse, or should we ride out and search for survivors?"

The sheriff shrugged, "Didn't sound like there'd be none. I was going out to check on things. Might be that a posse would be the best thing but guess that would be the territorial marshall would do that. We'll go out and look around and I'll get back to you." Jack noted that Thatcher, as he turned away and out of Tolliver's sight, was rolling his eyes.

The sheriff stopped and said to Jack, "Wait for me back at the office. I've got a couple of things to see to and then we can leave for the ranch."

Jack nodded and crossed the street to the jail where he sat down to wait. He had a notion that the sheriff was buying the story as strange but good enough. He would feel better just riding off to Longstreet but might as well see this through to the end. That should come soon enough. His thoughts wandered back to the doctor's daughter and a picture tried to form in his mind but he really couldn't make sense of it. There must be a lot of things that he just didn't know or understand. He thought about Amy and wished that he could talk to her about this. He had a hunch that she could explain all this stuff. Jack shook his head to clear it as he reminded himself that she was a married woman who was likely dead.

He felt like he was getting a little dizzy sitting there in the sun with no breakfast in him. He needed some food and a beer to wash it down. He roused himself and walked over to the hotel for some grub.

When Jack returned the sheriff was waiting with a deputy call Everet. Introductions over, they mounted and hit the road to the ranch. They rode for a while in silence but the sheriff, after urging Everet to scout ahead a little, cleared his throat noisily and started in, "Might as well get a few things out in the open, McGill, and the first thing is that there have been stories circulating about you since you shot up those two here in town.

By the sounds of things, you're quite a gun hand for a cowpuncher. You should know that I checked in on Martha and she told me about your wounded arm. She's some woman, isn't she? Got about twice the balls that Tolliver's got." The sheriff exploded in laughter at his own joke.

"I surely don't know what to make of Martha, and probably never will, but Tolliver is a yellow bellied son of a bitch, and that's for sure. Like hell I'm going to whistle up a posse cause some rich asshole out of my jurisdiction got robbed and murdered. I'll tell you, McGill, the old man Wilson had a hand in my getting this job. I needed work and that's a fact. Times are tough and I've kicked around a lot, even a little lawdog stuff way back, and maybe an assortment more questionable stuff. But now I'm the sheriff and I try to do that job the best I know how.

"I'm sure Tolliver thinks that the country is rising up and robbing and killing rich bastards but probably slim chance of that. From your account it sounds like Wilson was a target of some guys who knew what they were doing and got it done. You'd have to wonder if Tolliver is sitting on a pile of Wilson's money and if he'll be losing that to some long lost relative.

"By the way, McGill, I talked to Martha mostly for my own curiosity. As nasty as your account of Grady and Wilson is, it sort of squares with what I know of them. They were both mean, vicious men who probably enjoyed the hell out of hurting people. There's fellows like that cause I've seen it myself. Don't know just what makes them the way they are but think that they are better off dead, and probably better sooner than later.

"Well, sometimes I don't sound like much of a lawman but that's enough bullshit out of me. Why don't you entertain me with some stories of your gunslinging adventures."

Jack yawned loudly and grinned. "I wouldn't want to bore you, Sheriff. We'll see if I'm as good at entertaining as I am at getting bushwhacked." He showed the sheriff his wrists again and laughed. "The thing I'm most interested in, Sheriff, is getting back to Longstreet and checking in on my partner and maybe my girlfriend."

The sheriff tried to wring Jack for some tidbits of information but didn't really feel like he was having much luck. Time passed though and they finally reached the Wilson ranch. The embers of the house were still smoldering but the open safe was the only thing that could be clearly identified

The blaze had done a thorough job on the bodies. They couldn't get very close as the heat and the smell of the blackened corpses was very intense. The sheriff backed up shaking his head and gulping in fresher air. "Damn, ain't that something and a hell of a way to go. Guess that's the four of 'em. Sure ain't no way to tell any different.

"Where the hell do you suppose that round up camp is at? Guess maybe I should ride out that way and give 'em the news.

Those poor bastards will be out of a payday which won't put them in a very good mood."

They rode around the buildings one last time and the Sheriff turned to face Jack, "The hell with this, McGill. There's nothing here but what you said and that empty safe in the middle of the fire. We got to get out to that round up camp. Good luck finding your friends down south. It's been a pleasure meeting you." They shook hands and the two lawmen headed north while Jack struck out on the road to where he'd last seen Stretch.

Part V

Longstreet

It wasn't that hard to find Stretch's camp. The driver himself was farther up the hill in good cover with the gold, keeping an eye on the camp. It was almost dusk as he joined Jack at the fireside. The welcoming grin on his face was genuine.

Stretch pumped the fist that held the rifle and said, "Now ain't you a sight for sore eyes. There's some bacon and biscuits when you're ready and some whiskey in any event. I ain't gonna lie to you, McGill. It's good to see you made it."

Jack laughed and reached for the bottle. "Yeah, I made it, I guess. The sheriff certainly seemed satisfied with the mess we left at the ranch home place. It was still too hot to touch, but the bodies were pretty well scorched and burnt up. I want to see what happened in Longstreet and then I'm thinking that it might be best to get out of this part of the country. Think that it's time to start a new life somewhere else. What do you think?" He took a pull on the bottle and smiled at the quality of the whiskey.

Stretch laughed at Jack's expression as he reached for the bottle. "I know. I've never tasted anything that fine. It goes down too easy so I had one shot and then just left it alone. I guess that it seemed like a good idea to keep some of my wits about me.

"Think I agree with you about making tracks out of this country. Don't know what the hell to do but maybe I can buy into a hauling business or some other. I've never had to make decisions about that sort of thing. Don't really remember ever doing anything but just stumbling along into the next thing that happened. There's a hell of a lot to think about, so I've been trying to do some thinking. I watched the way you planned that fire back at the ranch so I know that you are used to thinking. I believe that you could teach me some things, if you got the time."

Jack thought about that but wasn't sure what to say. "I think I know what you're talking about but let's relax for now and sleep on it. So, did you get around to counting the money?"

"My numbers ain't much better than my planning, so I got up to a thousand and then about twenty thousand and then I just gave it up. Think it might be too much to count." He shrugged uneasily at the look he saw on Jack's face.

"Stretch, ole buddy, I thought about it a little. Put some wood on the fire, go get the money and let's get to the lessons."

Jack took another pull on the bottle and corked it while he helped himself to the bacon and biscuits. He taught Stretch a little simple math as they counted the money into two piles of a bit more than seventy-six thousand each and then just sat back and looked at all that money. Stretch managed to say, "Jesus H. Christ…". They each filled a saddlebag, had another drink, banked the fire and bunked down for the night full of their own thoughts.

They broke camp early and pushed the horses steadily to the southwest and Longstreet. Jack killed time on the trail and around the fire at night trying to school his partner as requested. He remembered some books and poems that his folks had read to him and his sister and brother. He told about books he'd read himself and heard about. He did the best he could with math and he showed Stretch the numbers and letters. Jack found that he rather enjoyed the effort, in great part because the hauler was eager to learn and asked a lot of questions. Jack was surprised at how much he was able to remember, especially the poems.

Midmorning on the third day they rode into Longstreet and made straight for the doctor's office. Jack dismounted and rapped on the door. The doctor recognized him and seemed relieved to see him. "Folks around here had about given you up for lost, McGill. Your partner Elmer is still trying to get mended up over at the hotel. He's a strong fellow and he might get almost back to his old self. He's going to be awful glad to see you as he still talks about you every day."

Jack smiled at that and asked the hard question next, "What about the girl, the girl who got shot up that day I disappeared from here? I got bushwacked and she got shot, I believe in the shoulder."

The Doctor did a double take at that question. There might have been a ghost of a twinkle crept into his eye. "Well, damn all, McGill. I knew there had to be a connection. I mean, I didn't have no proof and she never said a thing. But when they brought her here all covered with blood, they carried along all her stuff from the hotel room where they found her. The money belt with over two thousand dollars attracted a lot of attention. The bullet just scraped the bone and bruising was and still is quite extensive, but she is healing nicely.

"So the next day her old man showed up all in a dither about his beloved young wife and exclaims over her and vows revenge and whatnot and then asks about the bill. Well, I said that was no problem with that money belt for surety. And right then is when things started to fall apart and his mood went right to hell along with all those fine feelings he'd been expressing."

Jack broke in here, "Well, was she awake? What was she saying about the money and all?"

The doctor continued in a thoughtful tone. "You might as well know that I'm not the sort of man who defends infidelity or such goings on but the woman would only say that she was holding the money for a friend and the husband worked himself into a rage and started in threatening her…and she's already hurt and she's my patient.

"He was yelling and making like he was going to strike her and I pulled my pistol out of the drawer and leveled it at his belly. I told him I'd put him down like a mad dog if he laid a hand on my patient and I meant it. He was in a killing rage but I had the drop on him and was damn angry myself. I don't think that woman was the least bit afraid of him."

The doctor grinned and continued, "The husband backed down though he called her and me some downright awful names before he stormed out of here. Heard later that he caught up with the circuit judge at the hotel and filed for divorce and lit a shuck out of town with his new stock. It was more than enough excitement for me, I hope to tell you. I checked in on young Amy and your friend Elmer this morning at the hotel and that's where you'll find them."

Jack wasn't trying to hide his relief at the doctor's revelations. "Thanks Doc, I got to run now but I will send a bottle of the best whiskey in town if you'll have it." They shook hands on that, and Jack ran for his horse. Minutes later he and Stretch were tying up at the hitchrail in front of the hotel.

The first thing that Jack saw was Elmer sitting in a chair on the boardwalk smiling a welcome. "Well now, damned if it ain't my old partner come a'calling. I been wondering just what the hell had happened to you. Now don't wring that mitt very hard. I'm still in the mending process."

Jack motioned to Stretch. "This fellow that goes by the name of Stretch used to be at cross purposes with me but then he changed his mind and saved my life. Reckon that makes him a pretty good friend. I sure am glad to see you up and around, Elmer. I had cause to worry about you making it after that shootout with the Weaver gang."

Elmer brushed by that, saying, "You've got a story to tell about how in the hell you bagged all those fellows. I can't remember shit except that I was getting shot to pieces."

"If you can't remember a thing then I guess you're going to have to believe anything I tell you," Jack said with a grin. "But first I have to find a young woman who got shot and is staying here too. I don't suppose you'd happen to know her, would ya?"

Elmer nodded knowingly, "I do know young Amy and believe that you will find her in the dining room with her book." He winked and hooked his thumb towards the eatery.

Jack was standing at her table and studying the bandage bump on her left shoulder before she looked up and saw him. A smile spread across her face as she set the book aside.

"Well hi, Jack. I've been hoping you'd stop in and say hello." Her eyes were boring into him like he was a ghost and she indicated that he should sit. "Would you like some coffee and something to eat? You look kind of hungry."

They both laughed at that. Jack sat and tried not to devour her with his eyes. Finally he said, "I had quite a chat with the doc who patched you up. Is there still a lot of pain?"

She shrugged, "It's less every day and even better the last minute." She reached over and looked at the fading scars on his wrists. "I'm not going to go on about the things I've been thinking. I'm just glad you're here and that you have that crazy look in your eyes. I don't know if you need to eat but you definitely could use a shave and shower before you come up to visit number sixteen. Don't be all day!" She winked and took off with her book in hand and one little backward smile.

Amy fetched up with the blood draining out of her face as Stretch appeared in the doorway. The terror on her face caused him to throw up both hands immediately. He mumbled, "Sorry, Ma'am, and I'm with him now," as he gestured towards his new partner.

Amy looked back at Jack who nodded and said, "It's a long story. That's for later."

She headed for the stairs while Stretch joined Jack at the table. They decided to stash the saddlebags in the hotel safe and meet later. Jack set off to look for a bath and shave. A short time later he was rapping on Amy's door holding a couple of flowers he'd grabbed in the hotel lobby.

They enjoyed an emotional and exhausting reunion. A couple of hours later Jack felt the need for some food and he dragged himself out of Amy's bed and started dressing. She sat up in bed and watched him awhile before saying, "We really have to talk. What are we going to do, or what am I going to do? Are we a team or…? You don't have to say nothing right now but my life is sort of at a crossroads here and I am kind of wondering."

Jack was standing there watching her as he buttoned his shirt. He cleared his throat a little and said, "Not sure what to do.

You're alive, and then some, and I'm hungry. But, to tell the truth, even if it looks like I've got a knack for shooting bad guys, I'm not altogether sure that killing folks is the kind of business I want to be in over the long run. I was kind of thinking about looking into doctoring. I've been watching those fellows work and maybe that would be better than killing bad guys, you know."

"That is the craziest thing I ever heard," she exclaimed. "You're a cowhand and a bounty hunter and now you want to go off to school and be a medical man. Are you still thinking about this or is that mind of yours made up?"

Jack starred at her flashing eyes and nakedness and knelt by the side of the bed to gaze up at her. "If you tell me I can fly out the window, I can. If you tell me to do it right now, I will. On the other hand, if I go to school to learn some medicine I will need a good woman to take care of me and that sort of thing."

She bent towards him for a kiss and a caress and whispered, "Maybe we should think about this on a full stomach. But what I think I hear you saying is that we should form some sort of a partnership, you and I. You know that I still have to give that idea a lot of thought, even though it does have kind of a nice sound to it.

"I'm hungry too! What do you mean, anyway, by, '…that sort of thing.'? Would you consider sitting down to dinner in the hotel dining room with a divorced woman?"

Jack scooped her up out of the bed and kissed her hard. "Ma'am, I can't believe it took you this long to ask but in fact I can hardly wait to take you to dinner. Throw some clothes over your treasures and let's go eat!"

"Jack…Maybe I should call you honey? Anyway, when we can, as soon as we can, let's get out of this town. I can live with a little hard feeling, but I don't think that the minister's wife and her steamed up friends are ever going to get over the fact that

I was the one who got you into bed. I don't want to be a problem for you, Honey, but whenever you decide to leave I'll be more than ready."

Jack smiled as he helped the best he could with her buttons. "Got me into bed, huh? We'll have more on that later. As to the other, I am ready to move as soon as you are ready to travel. Also, in that vein, got to talk to Stretch and Elmer. Maybe we should all sit down to dinner and see where things are. Let's go find those fellows and get something to eat."

They found Stretch and Elmer sitting in front of the hotel and then headed to the dining room for dinner. Jack got a table at some remove from the other diners and after ordering some beer he said "Elmer, I don't know how you're feeling about moving or the plans of either of you, but Amy and I are fixing to get on the move if the doctor will give her a clean bill to travel. We're planning to head south to catch a train for the east coast through Kansas City and St. Louis. What are you fellows thinking?

We've all got some money now to take off on a kind of new life, if that's what you got a mind to be about. I'm considering along the lines of maybe taking up the study of medicine. See if I can patch people up as good as I can cut 'em down."

There were some chuckles around the table. Elmer cleared his throat. "I like the idea of moving on," he said. "My days of being a stage detective are probably about over and done with. So if the doc says I can move, I'm ready to go. While you two are thinking about the East coast, Stretch and I have been kicking around the idea of a freight business down there between west Texas and the other coast. The winters in that part of the country won't be so hard on my old bones. I 'spect I'll be starting the trip in an ole buggy but if the doc says so, then I'm plenty ready."

Elmer pointed out that they had just as well travel together for awhile as all were headed south. "There's a pretty good road south about twenty-five miles on the other side of Wakefield. You remember, Jack, that town where we met up?"

Jack nodded in assent.

Amy drummed her fingers on the table and smiled sweetly. "I believe that I will do that part of the trip under the seat in Elmer's buggy or will wear a very heavy disguise. I have more than a few memories of that town and surrounding countryside. There are also some acquaintances that I would not care to revisit."

Jack bowed slightly in what appeared to be mock remorse and reached for her hand. "We'll find some old clean clothes around town here and fashion you a very compelling disguise. I think that you'll look good as a stable hand."

She studied him coolly and grinned. "On reflection, I guess that I am not particular about that. The important thing is that I not be recognized and that you and I catch a train to Boston."

Jack thought Boston sounded pretty good, especially with her. "Let's just plan to spend very little time in Wakefield. We've got to talk to the doc and get some supplies together. Let's eat and then get to work. Stretch, pass me that beer, will ya?"

The doctor decided that Elmer should travel in a buggy for a least a week and then use his best judgment. It was decided that they would leave first thing in the morning. Stretch set off to find an old buggy with springs for Elmer. Jack went in search of a large tarp for a lean-to and a couple of camp cots. Amy's job was to find a disguise and start getting the food together. By evening they were almost ready to hit the road. They got together for dinner and final plans and were off to bed early.

Come morning, Amy tried on her new outfit. As she piled her long hair and pushed all of it under the old slouch hat she wrinkled her nose at her image in the mirror. She glanced sidelong at Jack who had a lecherous smile for her. He quickly assured her that she had never looked more beautiful and curvy than she did in those old clothes.

"Jack, there's no way you would have fallen for me if I'd looked like this on that fateful morning."

"Aw, darling, you are wrong, but we cannot recapture those magical moments. Come on, let's see if the boys can recognize you in your new duds."

They met downstairs for a big breakfast and final check of their supply list. Then Jack and Stretch were off to the livery for the buggy and all the horses. They got Elmer comfortable in the rig with his pillows and stowed the rest of the gear, which included a big basket of fried chicken, boiled eggs and beer from the hotel for traveling food. It was decided the Stretch and Jack would take turns driving the buggy so Elmer could ride resting and heal better. Amy was much better and could rein her pony with little problem. They moved out and set a steady pace into the rising sun.

Part VI

Wakefield

It would be a long journey but they were not going to rush

for time, and there was a good measure of things to plan and

think about. They fell into an easy camaraderie as they deepened

their acquaintances and looked to the future. On the afternoon of

the third day Jack raised one hand and brought his mount to a

halt. He pulled his rifle and pointed the attention of his

companions towards a small flock of turkeys a couple of hundred yards away towards the trees. Jack started to take aim when Amy kneed her horse forward into him and spoke in a low voice.

"Just a second there, my cowboy lover, and give your girl a chance to strut her stuff with a rifle." Jack gave her a skeptical look as she pulled her rifle and very carefully nestled it against her injured shoulder. It took her a minute to get it just right as she pulled up the bottom corner of her coat for more padding. Then she nodded at Jack and winked before she sighted down the barrel.

The big tom had taken a great interest in them by now and pushed his head higher. Suddenly his head exploded in blood as the rifle's crack rent the lazy afternoon. Amy gave the rifle a bit of dusting on her coat sleeve before returning it to the saddle scabbard. Her face was wreathed in a lovely and innocent smile. There was no hint of pride but only a gracious acceptance of her own skillfulness.

"Jack, my darling," she said, "would you mind fetching yonder bird for our supper. You're so nice and strong and he does look like a very big tom."

"Hot damn," Stretch yelled as the hen turkeys fled into the trees.

Elmer was shaking his head. "Where in the hell did you learn to shoot like that, young lady? I do believe that you could find a job in a carnival as a trick shooter. I'm quite sure I've never seen finer shooting."

Everyone was starring at her but she just laughed and lowered her eyes modestly.

Jack pushed up close to her and murmured in a low voice. "I believe that you might just be the woman I've been looking for." Then with a rebel yell of triumph he set off for the bird.

The turkey, chopped in pieces and slow roasted over the fire, was excellent. Amy withstood a lot of good-natured kidding about her marksmanship. She admitted that her father had started her on a rifle when she was very young and there had been plenty of time to practice during her short marriage to the sodbuster.

The following afternoon they were closing on Wakefield. Amy volunteered that she felt healthy enough to take the reins of the buggy for the ride through the town. She adjusted her hair and hat and climbed into the buggy seat with her rifle. Hunched in the heavy coat and covered by the old slouch hat she could have passed for a small boy. Everything seemed ready so they road into Wakefield and proceeded slowly down the main street.

The town was very quiet in contrast to all their anticipation. Jack raised his hand for a halt and came back to the buggy side. He pointed across the street at the mercantile and drawled, "Elmer, old friend, you really don't look like yourself lately without a cigar clamped in your teeth. Reckon I take a moment here and go grab a handful from the store over yonder."

Elmer grunted his surprise but raised no objection to the offer. Then Jack reached down and unbuckled his cartridge belt and hung it on the buggy seat. He winked at Amy and said, "I'm past tired of lugging that damned thing around and I reckon I can learn to live without it from now on. You watch my back, will you darling." Elmer snorted but just shook his head at Jack's decision.

Jack dismounted and tossed his reins to Stretch before crossing the road. He was almost to the boardwalk when he felt something moving up on him quickly from behind. Jack started to turn, instinctively raising his arm. He heard Stretch bellow a warning as a length of lumber smashed into his arm and the back of his head. As he fell forward he tried to roll as far as possible from his attacker. Jack knew he was hurt some but that the arm thrown up at the last second had saved him from the worst of the blow. His head was throbbing but he was conscious. He turned on one knee to confront his attacker. He had a hollow feeling in his stomach as he recognized the young fella with the ax handle.

"Now it's my turn, you son of a bitch," Jack's assailant snarled. "I can't believe you came back to my town. I'm gonna kill you deader then hell, you yellar bellied backshooter. You kicked me in the balls and now I'm going to shoot your balls right off ya and then I'm going to blow your brains all over this road. Stand up, you stinking coward!" With that the young tough threw the borrowed ax handle back towards the barrel on the boardwalk and grabbed the handgrip of his pistol.

A bystander in the mercantile doorway spoke up then. "He doesn't even have a gun on him, Rodgers. You shoot him and it will be murder!"

"You shut up, you son of a bitch. I'll kill you too, Schlutz, and don't doubt I will." He raised and lowered the pistol in the holster while glancing around wildly for a way to make this work out the way he had dreamed of since the day of his humiliation. The answer to all his prayers was within reach and he could not be cheated out of his revenge.

The kid suddenly glanced back at the fella in the doorway and saw the answer. He jerked out his pistol and brandished it at the man, yelling, "Throw him your pistol, Schlutz. You're so worried about him so throw him your gun. Do it now or I'm going to gun you first before I do him. Throw it out there in the dirt."

It was clear that the man did not want to comply with the kid's command, but the lad had the drop on him and a reputation that would give anyone pause. He had been nothing but a problem for as long as he'd been around. The man eased out his pistol and advanced a couple of steps before throwing it on the far side of and behind Jack.

Jack's head felt wooly but his vision had cleared and he clenched his fist to try his grip. He glanced behind him to the gun in the dirt and considered his chances. That glance had also revealed that Stretch was off his horse and advancing with his rifle.

The kid waved his pistol and moved a couple of steps out into the road. He chuckled and gestured towards the borrowed pistol. "I'm counting to five now and you better have a handful of that sixshooter when I get there." He pointed his pistol at Jack and said, "One, two, three…"

Jack rose to his feet slowly and took a step backwards and then another. He was watching the gun already leveled at his belly. He knew almost to a certainty that there was no good way out of this. Suddenly the kid's hand was spraying blood and a rifle barked and the handgun dropped unfired to the road. Time seemed to stop as the kid starred at his ruined hand and then he screamed in pain and rage. Jack glanced back across the road at the buggy. Amy was sitting there under the slouch hat, sighting down the barrel, waiting.

The kid was still screaming. He reached down suddenly with his left hand to get his pistol. When he grabbed it and tried to rise his knee jerked very hard as the rifle spoke again. Blood gushed down his leg from the collapsing knee. The pistol barrel was now driven into the dirt, the only support that kept him from falling face down in the road.

The kid's face was a mask of agony as he looked up and around him to see what had happened to ruin what had looked to be such a perfect day. He saw that his enemy still had not moved towards the gun in the dirt. Then he glanced across the road and saw what looked like a young boy in heavy clothes pointing a rifle right at him. He knew that that must be the shooter but wondered why some young boy in a buggy would be shooting him full of holes.

Jack noticed movement to the rear of the buggy and recognized the town sheriff standing there with his hand on his gun butt. It appeared like he was letting the thing play out before announcing his presence.

The kid tried to focus as the shooter made a motion with the rifle to throw his gun away. The pain of his wounds and the rage in his heart seemed to be too much for the lad as he lurched backwards. He pulled the gun barrel out of the dirt and snapped off a shot towards the buggy. But it was a left-handed attempt and the pistol barrel was jammed full of dirt. It blew apart as he fired. The damage to his hand and lower belly looked to be considerable as he lay back on the road in a dead faint.

Amy raised the rifle, resting the butt on her thigh as the sheriff moved forward into her line of sight. He walked over to look down at the kid and shook his head at the bloody mess. He looked around and spied a little fella looking out the door of the mercantile. He motioned him over and sent him off for the doctor. Then the old lawman turned his attention to Jack and nodded him over in the direction of the buggy. They walked over together.

The sheriff saw Elmer and rolled his eyes. "I thought I seen the last of you birds. McGill, what in the devil are you doing, walking around here without a gun? My town ain't changed all that much these last few weeks. You must know that you've got quite a reputation by now, and it's growing all the time. I do have to say, Elmer that you are a sight for sore eyes. I'd been hearing that you got shot to pieces way out northwest and didn't make it."

"Now who is this young fellow here doing the fancy shooting?" The sheriff took a breath and glared at the youth on the seat in front of him with head downward under the slouch hat and rifle pointed skyward. He cleared his throat and reached at the hat when the head tilted back and the lovely face came into view. Amy smiled prettily at him and then dropped her chin again.

"Howdy, Sheriff," came her voice from hiding.

The sheriff coughed or tried to and glanced around to both sides to see if there were any close watchers. Satisfied, he spoke a hoarse whisper. "I do believe that I am confronted here with the former wife of James Brenner, one of our local sodbuster homesteaders. I've only seen her once before but she was mighty fetching and hard to forget. Word around is that her ex-husband is having a hard time forgetting also, and has been heard to make threats upon her life should any opportunity ever present itself.

"I think that for starters you might put the rifle down and give the reins to Elmer if he fit enough." Elmer nodded that he was up to it and took the reins.

The lawman glanced at Stretch and then back to Jack, who was busy buckling on his gun. "What are you gents up to, McGill? I sure hope you're just passing through. No offense."

Jack gave him a wry grin and said, "We'd like to stay and see what the rest of the day has to offer but there's a long trip ahead so we'd better git along down the road. Hell of it is that we just stopped for a handful of cigars and I plumb forgot about that damn kid with the sore crouch. Thanks, sheriff, and take care or yourself."

Jack mounted and reached for his reins as the sheriff nodded and stepped away from the buggy.

The sheriff held up his hands for Jack's attention and said, "Good luck, McGill. I still owe you one from before so take your time leaving town and I'll send some lad on the run to catch you with that handful of cigars." He waved his farewell.

A couple hours out of town they passed the turnoff to Brenner's place. There was no sign of life and soon it was well behind them. After a while Amy called a stop to mount her horse. She'd said little since the incident in town and obviously wasn't very happy. She glowered at Jack and insisted that she examine the welt on the side of his head. He suffered quietly like a real gentleman through her attentions and ill humor.

He ventured, "That's another good reason why I need you so much, darling, so's you can tell me when I should wear a gun and when I needn't. Now, can I see a smile or are you going to save all your smiles for Boston?"

She glared at Jack as hard as she could manage and then pushed up close to put her arm around him. They were both smiling as they rode down the coach road together.

13182288R00112

Made in the USA
Charleston, SC
21 June 2012